NICOLE WAS
THEIR HOMECOMING QUEEN

DR. MARCEL BEAUREGARD
The headmaster lived up to his title in unexpected ways.

DR. RODERICK DUNCAN
His Elizabethan tongue did more than speak English to Nicole.

CODY CAMERON
Nicole's alluring rival became her very intimate friend.

TOMMY RIDDLE
His kinky cosmetics made people kiss and make up.

MAKE IT TO NICOLE'S REUNION . . .
IT ONLY COMES ONCE!

Nicole's
REUNION
Morgan St. Michel

A JOVE BOOK

NICOLE'S REUNION

A Jove Book / published by arrangement with
the author

PRINTING HISTORY
Jove edition / September 1983

ISBN: 0-515-07132-3

Jove books are published by The Berkley Publishing Group,
200 Madison Avenue, New York, N.Y. 10016. The words
"A JOVE BOOK" and the "J" with sunburst are trademarks
belonging to Jove Publications, Inc.

PRINTED IN THE UNITED STATES OF AMERICA

for Jaclyn
with passion

chapter one

It had not been my first orgasm, but it had been my best. For that reason alone, the Académie Dumont would live in my memory forever. On its sun-dappled campus on the outskirts of Paris, the air crisp with autumn and fragrant with the nutty aroma of crunchy leaves, I began my last year succumbing to the sweet smell of *suck*cess at the hands and mouth of the girl who was to become my closest and dearest friend ever, Gilda Morrow.

How glorious it had been! How indescribably thrilling, how utterly euphoric! The mere remembrance of it was capable of summoning my smoldering sensuality to instant climactic tribute. I came again for just that reason as I read the engraved invitation which had just arrived at the Castle von Hoffman addressed to me by my full (ugh!) name, Nicole Marie Thérèse Louise de Savoie-Carignan LaSalle:

You are most cordially invited to attend a special *"Decade at Dumont"* homecoming reunion celebration for graduates of the past ten years during the week of Sept. 7–14.

> (signed) Dr. Marcel Beauregard,
> Headmaster.

Nostalgia enveloped me after I had come for joy. My first encounter with Gilda had been memorable and outstanding, but there were many, many more moments of happiness and erotic fantasy to recall from my years at the Académie as well. The memories came like multiple orgasms as I reflected on the happy days at Dumont, my eighteenth birthday, and my final, glorious year there.

As if alerted by telepathy, Gilda called in the midst of my reverie. She was in Rio—once again deeply involved with her Brazilian millionaire playboy.

"Did you get it?"

"I get it whenever I want it," I jibed.

"Not *that*," she sniffed, deflated by my flippancy. "The invitation, I mean."

"I get a dozen of those a day." I continued being evasive just for the hell of it.

"Nicole!" she screeched in frustration. "I'm talking about a reunion invitation from the Académie!"

"Oh, *that?*" I feigned nonchalance. "Yes, I got it."

"And you're not excited about it?" she asked in disbelief. "After all the times we talked about how great it would be?"

"Nostalgia's for old people. We've been out of school only a few years."

"I don't want to believe your attitude," she said almost scornfully.

"Why?"

"I haven't seen you in six or seven weeks, and you've changed completely. All of a sudden, you're no longer sweet and sexy, but blasé and jaded."

I couldn't maintain my indifferent pose any longer. Knowing Gilda, she was liable to hang up on me if I continued to harpoon her happiness, which I shared completely—though not obviously to her.

"If that's the way you feel"—I began grimly, then exploded dramatically—"then I want you to know that I think it's just about the most wonderful thing to happen since God invented fucking—so how do you like that, young lady!?"

Gilda whooped and hollered clear across the Atlantic and half of Europe.

"You bitch!" she shrieked. "You gorgeous, lying little bitch stringing me on like that!"

Laughter tangled up my words and eventually choked them off altogether. We must have giggled and hooted and laughed and cried away the price of an excellent bottle of champagne before we were able to resume conversing on anything approaching coherence.

"Where will I meet you?" I was finally able to ask intelligibly.

"How about Paris?"

"Aunt Valerie's?"

"Why not? I haven't seen that exotic neurotic in months. She's always fun."

"Call me the week before the reunion," I suggested. "Then we'll get the exact times set."

"As you command, Your Highness."

"Go fuck yourself," I retorted amiably.

"My finger has already begun following your instructions," Gilda said in mock subservience.

"While you come, I'll go."

3

"Love you, babe," she cooed.

"Love you, too. It'll be a great reunion."

I hung up and then returned the receiver—not to its cradle but to the cradle of my cunt. It was like having Gilda there, communicating over the miles to my libido. As I climaxed blissfully, visions of the homecoming and the fantasy fulfillment it promised danced across the stage of my mind. I hadn't been this full of happy anticipation in years. It was a beautiful feeling, and I fell asleep with all of it—including the telephone—clutched to my bosom.

chapter two

Little did it matter where or when I fell asleep at
the castle—more often than not, I wound up sandwiched between Count Erich and Countess Ulrica
von Hoffman in their huge canopied bed, ulti-
mately to be awakened by a combination of his
morning manhood between the cheeks of my
derrière and the fresh velvet of her tongue inside
the cove of my cunt. It was a delightful way to be
ushered into a new day, and once the pulsing passion had restored me to full consciousness, I
reciprocated in my own inimitable fashion, orally-
ing to the cause of causing climaxes from both of
them.

"Good, good, good morning to you, darling
Nicole," Erich chattered cheerfully as Ulrica
deftly blotted the residue of silky come from the
crown of his cock. "I trust you slept well?"

I turned a lazy yawn into a warm smile. "I
awakened even better."

ce, wasn't it?'' Ulrica
ght stimulation to whet
ast, don't you think?''

its rose like twin ships on a
bowsprits.

more happiness in the world if
the day that way,'' I concurred.
for champagne and fruit?'' the
as he slipped into a maroon robe.

, Erich,'' Ulrica demurred. ''Since
she'll ving shortly, Nicole and I planned to
picnic in the meadow. She hasn't ridden once yet
on this visit.''

"You didn't tell me that,'' I responded. ''But I
like the idea. I wonder if Cocaine misses me.''

The countess laughed. ''Not half as much as the
chief groom,'' she teased.

"Oh, yes, Gunther,'' I recalled. ''Don't tell
him, but I'd actually almost forgotten about
him.''

"That would be a devastating bit of news to
him, I'm sure,'' Erich said. ''Every time he
brushes down that pure white coat of Cocaine's,
I'm certain he's entertaining impure thoughts
about the horse's favorite rider.''

"Impetuous, maybe, but not impure,'' I
replied.

"Of course not.'' Ulrica sided with me. ''I'm
surprised at you, Erich. There's nothing impure in
being impassioned—as you well know and understand.''

The count flung his hands toward the ceiling. ''I
well know I stand corrected. I was thinking of
semen when I should have been thinking of
semantics.''

"You're forgiven.'' I flicked his cock as it
peeked from the folds of his robe.

"He's always difficult in the morning," Ulrica said chidingly.

"I'm like most men. I find it hard getting up."

"But never hard getting *it* up, right?" I jested.

"Never."

The countess had been busying herself assembling a wardrobe for the day's outing.

"Come, come, you two," she said with feigned impatience, "are we going to banter or canter?"

"Count me out," Erich announced as though he had been included in the planning. "I have an important meeting with my estate manager."

"Count the count out," I kidded, assuming the pose of a boxing referee over the body of a floored fighter. "One . . . two . . . three . . . four . . ."

"It's you who should go down for the count," he jibed, flashing his revitalized cock by fanning out the sides of his robe like wings. "After all, it's you who are leaving, not Ulrica or I."

Without further ado, I knelt before him and fed his swollen prick to my mouth. I could feel it tremble against the surface of my palate.

"At this rate, we'll never get started," Ulrica complained, standing next to us with her arms akimbo.

"I'll come fast," Erich promised. "Nicole has a way of inspiring quick responses."

I fluttered my eyelashes at her as she shook her head in mock exasperation. We both knew that a cardinal rule of life around the castle was that nothing—*nothing*—took precedence over any sexual activity whatever.

"Save a few drops for family obligations," Ulrica reminded him as she turned away to resume getting ready for the ride.

"Always, my dear."

Moments later, his cock performed like a smoking gun, spewing bullets of oysterish come down my throat, against the roof of my mouth and onto my gaping lips.

"Hallelujah!" Erich grunted contentedly after the last shot had been fired. "You've given me something to remember you by, sweet little Nicole."

"What?" Ulrica chimed in, "an antique pistol with all empty chambers?"

The count clutched his still-swollen prick menacingly. "You wait and see what happens to you tonight, my lady of the fiery loins," he declared with mock anger. "You had better sleep with one eye open if you know what's good for you."

"I will," Ulrica promised with a smile. "The one between my legs."

The count boomed with laughter, and the two of us joined in, hugging one another in the affectionate way that had made my life at the castle such a joyous one. Real anger was hard to come by anywhere on the sprawling premises, but good-natured verbal jousting was as common as clover throughout the castle and estate grounds.

"I'm getting out of here while I still have my sanity," Erich declared, backing through the double doors of the bedroom.

"Too bad you didn't do that while you still had your virility," Ulrica needled him.

"Good-bye, ladies," he said as the doors parted to swallow him. "Harangue the horses for a change."

Once he was gone, Ulrica got down to business quickly and efficiently. "The penis is a very obtrusive organ. See how nicely and rapidly we get things done without having one poking around?"

"They are good company at times, though," I put up a phallic defense.

Ulrica stopped what she was doing. "Granted, but if you had a choice, which would you prefer for yourself?"

I paused momentarily. "I've been so fortunate with what I have, I'd be a fool not to stick with it."

She smiled knowingly. "You'll get no argument from me. In the end, it's worth all the bother and the blood."

"Let's not get clinical, or I might change my mind," I responded kiddingly.

"Not after the surprise I have for you in the meadow."

I nudged her inquisitively. "Little Boy Blue's going to blow his horn?"

"No," she replied, "and you're not going to blow it either."

"Tell me."

"Wait and see."

"You're getting me hot," I warned.

"Good! You look even more tempting that way."

I pouted. "It's not fair to keep me in the dark."

"You'll be in bright sunshine when it happens," she assured me.

I decided not to press her further for details. The anticipation was almost like masturbation to my libido. I loved secret sex, especially the kinky kind Ulrica enjoyed arranging when Erich was absent.

"Pardon me, countess," a voice sounded from behind the double doors. "I have the picnic lunch you requested from the kitchen last evening."

"Oh, yes, André," she replied. "Bring it in, please."

A white-uniformed steward, cocoa-skinned and immaculate, came gingerly through the entrance bearing a large wicker basket, its contents wrapped in a red-checkered tablecloth. It smelled delicious even from a distance.

"Ummmmmm," I murmured, licking my lips.

André smiled shyly at me, then placed the basket on the bed.

"Thank you," Ulrica said to him.

"My pleasure, Countess," he replied, sneaking another look at my scantily clad body before retreating.

"He's cute," I observed after he'd gone.

"Loves to suck," Ulrica revealed offhandedly. "Ring the kitchen and try him sometime."

"Right now the aroma from that basket is even more tempting," I said sincerely.

"The chef does an especially excellent job on these outdoor lunches. I often go alone to the meadow and just loll the afternoon away sipping wine and munching on the goodies he concocts for me."

"Does he also cunt-cock for you?" I played on her words.

"I'll never tell," she replied, winking.

We took a jeep to the stables where Gunther awaited us. "You've been here for over a week and haven't been riding once," he accused me with a smile.

I skipped over to him and planted an open-mouthed kiss over his lips. His cock literally leaped inside the cage of his jeans.

"How could I possibly forget two such beautiful stallions as Gunther and Cocaine?" I teased him.

"He's five-legged, and I'm only three-legged," he responded with just a tinge of embarrassment.

"You've got hands to make up the difference," I suggested sultrily. It was all game-playing on my part this time since I had no particular desire at the moment to utilize Gunther for anything beyond saddling and calming my mount.

"Rogue looks restless this morning," Ulrica observed, eyeing her handsome palomino stallion.

"He's a little frisky," Gunther agreed, obviously reluctant to return to shoptalk after being aroused. "He'll be okay once you get on him."

"Just like a man," I noted jokingly.

The countess seemed more anxious than usual to get the stable chitchat over and done with so that we could get under way.

"Gunther if you will, please hand me the basket in the jeep once I'm up on Rogue," she requested.

"Certainly," he said.

We took off shortly after, leaving a clearly disappointed chief-groom behind.

"I think he thought we might go for a bit of fun and games again, didn't you?" I questioned when I was able to catch up to the fleet-footed palomino.

Ulrica smiled knowingly. "Definitely, but I have other things in mind."

"What a devilish, scheming mind it is, too," I flicked my tongue from the corner of my mouth. Ulrica's eyes danced in response.

"I hope you'll come back after the reunion," she said, changing the subject.

"You know me, Ulrica. I have no definite plans, ever."

"Peter called. Did anyone tell you?"

"No, but that's all right. I'm not planning to contact him until after the homecoming. Anyhow, he's busy now with some financial transaction."

"And Gilda?"

I looked at her directly, keeping my eyes locked with hers despite the movements of our horses. "We are going to have the greatest, wildest, fucking and sucking time imaginable," I announced with utmost conviction.

"I envy you." Ulrica seemed delighted nonetheless.

"I'll have to come back just to tell you about it," I said.

The countess was quiet and pensive for a time as we waded through a sea of baa-ing sheep.

"Maybe something can be arranged," she said finally and cryptically.

I might have questioned her further if it hadn't been for the sheep ambush.

"How do we get them to leave us alone?" I asked, becoming claustrophobic in the midst of an entire herd.

"The dogs will drive them away. I just don't want to call them until we've picked our picnic spot. Erich's planning to thin the herd this fall. It's just grown too large for the grazing grounds."

We both settled on an almost perfect location for our repast; a clump of evergreens distinguished by a craggy outcropping of dark rock and a patch of vividly green grass that resembled a magic carpet thrown there by Mother Nature for our enjoyment. The sheep shied away from it as though they understood that it was intended only for the use of a higher form of life.

"Beautiful," I declared as we dismounted and tied our horses to a pair of stately trees.

"It's the most attractive spot on the entire estate," Ulrica said. "Look, you can see the castle from here—way in the distance."

I shaded my eyes and skimmed them over the rolling terrain. "You're right. It looks almost like a mirage."

"Sometimes I think it is," Ulrica laughed.

We spread out the checkered cloth together and began delving into the neatly wrapped foil packages and containers of food. There were nuggets of lobster and crabmeat, cold breast of capon, silvery herring and a pungent pâté, freshly baked bread and rolls, divine relishes and tarragon-dressed vegetable slivers—all accompanied by two full bottles of Beaujolais and a small carafe of liqueur for after dining. In such an atmosphere of idyllic grandeur, the food was almost orally sensual, the eating of it similar to performing fellatio or cunnilingus. I reveled in every bite and sip.

"Let's strip," Ulrica suggested midway through.

"Good idea," I agreed readily.

We accomplished our disrobing quickly and resumed dining with gusto. I was not so enraptured by the food as not to notice again what a marvelously voluptuous figure the countess possessed. As she sat down, she plumped her tits as though they were pillows—and well they might have been.

"Is my surprise coming soon?" I asked as I devoured a black olive in one succulent gulp.

"Yes, and so will you be."

"I have no reason—based on past experience with you—to doubt that at all."

"You won't be disappointed," she assured me.

A bit later on, when we were midway through the second bottle of wine, Ulrica went over to her horse, petted him briefly, and then took out a small, slender cylinder from a saddle compartment. Holding it up toward me, she asked, "Know what this is?"

"Nose candy?" I guessed.

"No, not cocaine. That's your horse. It's a whistle."

"And you're going to blow it?" I asked.

"It and what responds to it."

"I don't get it."

"You will, and you'll love it."

The sound was very shrill and high-pitched,

almost inaudible, really. I watched her as she looked over the immediate horizon in the direction the sheep had gone. Only moments later, a majestic-looking dog with long sable and white fur appeared on the crest of a hill, his eyes searching for the source of the sound.

"Jomar!" Ulrica called out.

The dog—a collie, I could see now—swooped down the hill toward us in a blur of motion. He ran up to the countess immediately, panting heavily. I watched as he burrowed his angular muzzle in her naked crotch.

"Naughty boy!" she scolded, laughing. "You're just as bad as your master."

"All dogs love to sniff, it seems," I noted. "Don't tell me you're into dogs now?"

She looked at me curiously. "He's handsome enough, isn't he?" she teased. "But no, it's his owner we're after."

"You're after," I corrected. "I don't even know him—or her."

"It's a him. He should be coming along any moment now that Jomar's here."

The dog had wandered over to sniff my snatch in the interim. "I'm being identified by my balling badge," I kidded.

"Remember, as a child, seeing dogs locked together in fucking?" Ulrica asked. "It was always such a strange, mysterious ritual."

"Especially when the horny male couldn't get out of the bitch," I recollected.

"Jomar's pedigreed, so he goes to bed only with the best," the countess said.

"I envy dogs the way they can just hop to it and get off anywhere they please," I commented. "They fuck in public whether the authorities are present or not."

"You come close to it yourself, Nicole," Ulrica

noted slyly. "Prying eyes never pried you apart from someone you wanted to seduce, no matter what the location."

"I exercise some restraint," I defended myself.

"Not as much as you exercise your vaginal muscles," she kidded, only partly in jest.

"Pussies need to stay in condition, just like athletes," I retorted.

"I think big Jomar is turning into a lapdog the way he hangs around your haunches," Ulrica observed.

I was about to respond when we were suddenly taken by surprise. Out of the evergreens, opposite from where the dog had come, emerged a strapping man, well over six feet, with imposing shoulders and a broad, pleasantly handsome face. He carried a shotgun loosely in one hand—but the most striking thing about him was the fact that here—in the Austrian foothills—he wore colorful plaid kilts, the short, pleated skirt of the Scottish Highlands. Even before he spoke, my curiosity had already wandered up his legs.

"Kingman, you cocksman!" Ulrica blurted out. "How dare you sneak up on two naked ladies without so much as a warning whistle?"

"Ulrica, lass," he responded with arms outstretched, "sure'n it's you—bare to the ass!"

They came together, kilt to cunt, as the dog left me to greet his master and the woman he'd begun masturbating.

"Ahem," I rasped, pretending to clear my throat.

The Scotsman very definitely had not forgotten my presence. I caught his mischievous eye over the shoulder of the countess, even as he toyed with her aroused cunt.

"I say there, Ulrica," he said loudly into her ear, "a fair maiden doth share the meadow with us—or else I'm the victim of heavenly hallucinations.''

They both turned to look at me now, a sun-dappled nymph with protruding pussy and nipples to match.

"Isn't she divine?" Ulrica commented. "Kingman MacLeod, this is my dear, sweet, darling Nicole."

"It is my extreme pleasure to meet you dear, sweet, darling Nicole," he repeated after her with rolling diction and rising dick.

"Shall I call you Mac or King?" I asked tantalizingly.

"Whichever proper or improper noun summons me to confront you directly," he replied with an openly lascivious look.

"Confront at the cunt front, Kingman MacLeod," I invited him with both given and surname.

"Hold my gun, please, Ulrica?"

"I prefer the one under the kilt," she declared.

"It will be yours to caress and fondle momentarily," he assured her as he strode toward me purposefully.

"Do you get tired of being asked if men wear anything under their kilts?" I asked as he drew up before me.

"Not when the interrogators are naked young women of incomparable beauty like you."

"Then what *do* you wear?" I asked impishly.

He lifted his skirt like a schoolgirl, an enormously erotic act when performed by a man of his muscular physique. I looked down to see nothing but a stunning cock that resembled a clenched fist and forearm rising from a scarlet fire. In fact, his whole body bristled with engaging reddish hair.

"You're wearing a hard-on!" I declared, clutching it immediately in both hands.

"Consider it a gift to both of you," he stated grandly.

"The Scots are known to be tight," Ulrica injected, "so take it before his native thrift gets the better of him."

"I'd prefer that both of you ladies be tight instead," he responded good-naturedly, "particularly in the slot for investments."

The kidding got serious in short order as the two of us took turns taking it dog-fashion from Kingman while his own dog worked out his amatory frustrations fucking the knothole of a fallen tree trunk. We laughed as we licked and fucked, enjoying the rollicking style and manner of the jovial Scot in and out of our slots. He had bought the estate adjoining the von Hoffmans' solely for the purpose of hunting game several times a year. The game obviously included as many females as his cock could gun down—aided, of course, by his trained canine assistant.

"I taught him to track pussy," Kingman confessed after we'd all had a temporary sufficiency of succulent sex. "He goes wild in the cities where that kind of game abounds."

Kingman and Jomar were long gone before we got off to sleep, our day's adventure igniting us both with such fires of passion that we went through Gunther, André, and Mimi, the maid, before ambushing Count Erich in the prize ring that constituted his four-poster bed. All in all, it amounted to good training for the rigors of reunion, I assured myself just before finally succumbing to the seductive charms of Morpheus.

chapter three

Amid the usual parting tears—no matter how often I left the count and countess, I could never overcome the tinge of sadness I felt upon saying good-bye to them—I held my hair against the stiff wind churned up by the rotor blades and boarded the count's helicopter for the flight to Vienna. From there to Paris I would go by jet. Once the castle and the waving arms in the courtyard were behind me, I managed quickly to regain my *joie de vivre* and the wondrous sense of anticipation that the prospect of a school reunion inspired within me.

The flight to Paris was on time and routine, allowing me to complete the reading of the final chapter of a novel, *The Adultery Commitment*, written by a Riviera friend of mine and rumored to be a thinly veiled depiction of my life. Having finished it, I could only be amused by the gossip. The central character was much too inhibited, much too sexually unimaginative ever to be Nicole. Still, the speculation had helped to make the book a best-seller not only in Europe but in the United States as well. That pleased me—if only for having added to the income of a witty and charming companion. I made a mental note to drop Charles Leroux a congratulatory message from Aunt Valerie's offices. He would probably be relieved to hear that, despite the publicity, I was amused rather than angered by all the cockeyed conjecturing.

As we circled for landing over the most beautiful of cities, my thoughts turned from *roman à clef* to Auntie Oolala. Aunt Valerie, by any form of measure, was truly something else. A kook she was, but also sensual and voluptuous in a uniquely original and subtle way. Her crazy act was really always under control, when I reflected on her bizarre twists and turns. She could meet the Queen of England and pass for a lady of distinction just as easily as she could spread her most private possession for a salivating army of males and females at an orgy. I loved her for her free spirit, her utter disdain for convention. Love was love, fuck was fuck, suck was suck. She never lost sight of the serpentine boundaries between them.

A new chauffeur was there to spirit me to her town house, a merry-eyed little man with closely cropped silver hair and a flashing neon smile.

"I had no trouble determining which person would be you, mademoiselle," he said as he grasped my matching bags from a revolving rack. "The description provided by your aunt was eminently correct."

"I'm afraid to hear it," I confessed.

"You won't," he replied with a wink. "Not from these lips, at any rate."

"That bad?" I kidded him.

"That good, in a perhaps slightly bad sort of way."

"You can trust me," I assured him.

"Thank you, Mademoiselle Nicole, but I don't know you well enough to be so bold in choice of words."

"What is your name?" I inquired as we forded through the throng cluttering the terminal.

"Roger."

"Roger, I absolve you from any responsibility whatsoever for what my Aunt Val said. You're merely acting as a conduit for her words."

"I don't know," he hesitated.

"Please?" I pleaded. "Auntie makes me laugh no matter what she says."

"You won't hold it against me?"

"I won't even make it hard for you," I reversed an old carnal cliché.

That apparently convinced him.

"She merely said I should look for the most beautiful, the most fuckable blonde imaginable and I would be looking at Nicole," he reported.

"Why, that was nothing at all to give you pause, Roger. I think that was a very sweet description from Auntie."

"As I said before, very accurate," he repeated.

I smiled at him. "How do you like working for a certified lunatic?" I joked.

"Mademoiselle Valerie is a very thoughtful and conscientious employer," he reported.

*Cunt*scientious, too, I thought to myself, but did not utter it.

"She's a dear," I agreed. "I don't suppose you know what her latest promotional passion involves, do you?"

"If you'll forgive me, I'll leave that to her to describe to you."

"Fine," I agreed. "She prefers it that way, I know from past experience."

Aunt Valerie's latest car was spectacular, a sleek saffron racing model unlike any I had ever seen before.

"My God!" I exclaimed. "What is it—from outer space?"

Roger stood by it proudly as though he had parented it—or at the least designed it.

"It's a Lamborghini Countach," he explained. "It cost your aunt two hundred thousand dollars."

"It looks it," I replied, not as fazed by the price as Roger seemingly had expected.

"Does it ever fly!" he reported with a touch of awe. "I'm used to navigating Rolls-Royces, Bentleys, and Mercedeses. I really have to watch my foot on the gas pedal with this."

A crowd stood around admiring the car and obviously trying to identify the blonde getting into it.

"Do you know any back roads where we can let it take off?" I inquired in a conspiratorial tone when we were ready to leave.

"I won't go over a hundred fifty kilometers," he informed me in all seriousness. "My heart won't take it."

I smiled reassuringly. "I was only kidding. I'll get Aunt Val to take me out one day. She's a frustrated Grand Prix driver at heart."

"It's not a car to be toyed with," he warned. "It's a very powerful animal."

"I love the daring of it," I purred as I rubbed its plush interior. "The color and design are almost vaginal."

He looked at me as if to say that my blood relationship with Valerie was becoming more and more apparent. But of course he said no such thing.

"If you'd like to take the wheel—" he suggested but with little enthusiasm.

"No, thank you, Roger," I responded. "I'd prefer to enjoy the ride in to the city without endangering both our lives."

"Whatever is your pleasure, mademoiselle," he replied.

Aside from the inevitable stares from passing motorists and pedestrians, as confused as I was regarding the identity of the model, the trip to the town house went smoothly and pleasantly. Roger amused me with stories about some of the strange and furtive types whom Aunt Valerie employed in her various foundations. By the time we arrived, I could hardly wait to greet my wacky but warm and wonderful Auntie.

Gushing from the mouth, arms outstretched and flailing, her curvy figure resplendent in a pink sheath that clung as closely to her as the lick of a tongue, Aunt Valerie swooped down the carpeted staircase into the vestibule of her building with a screech of greeting that sounded like a siren responding to some unknown emergency.

"Niiiiiccccooooooolllllleeee. . . !" she shrieked, holding the last syllable until it was finally cut off by the seal of her lips on mine.

"Aunt Val," I gasped when I was able to breathe again, "you act as though I'd returned from the dead."

"Oh, no, no, never," she denied emphatically. "You're the most alive and vital person on earth. It's just that I get so carried away with pride and happiness whenever I see you. To think that you've grown into such a stunning and brilliant young lady—my own little niece child—is such a source of satisfaction and achievement to me. You do understand, don't you, darling?"

How could I not smile in acknowledgment of such a tribute?

"I do, Auntie. It's sweet of you to think that way."

"The little girl I bounced on my knee," she reflected, her eyes sparkling.

"Now bounces on her own."

She looked at me directly, and now her eyes danced. "It was a good, full childhood."

"Are we going to spend the visit in the vestibule?" I inquired.

She laughed. "Oh, no, no, darling. Forgive me for getting carried away. I've been so moved, thinking about your coming to Paris for your reunion. Time is so dreadful in the way it speeds."

"Like your new car?" I suggested.

She giggled like a schoolgirl. "Isn't it sexy?" she asked rhetorically. "I just adore it."

"I'll have to baptize it before I leave," I proposed.

"Splendid idea, little one," she agreed with typical enthusiasm.

"Roger has my bags," I said.

"I'm sure they're already in your suite," she replied. "I've put you up on top this time."

"Top or bottom," I shrugged, "I enjoy myself equally."

She reached over and tweaked my cheek. "You delicious little vixen," she said. "Come, let's have a welcoming cocktail."

I followed her into the drawing room, past the grand piano she played only when she was high, and into the white-furnitured and green-ferned solarium. It was Aunt Val's favorite drinking room.

"Champagne, or something more wicked?"

"Champagne is fine," I replied. "I'll reserve the wickedness for later."

One of her housemen emerged as if by magic from the dense greenery, bearing a silver bucket crammed with ice and a smoking bottle of freshly opened champagne. He smiled shyly as he handed us each a glass and poured.

"Merci," I said, smiling back at him.

"A bit of caviar, too, please," Auntie instructed.

"Oui, mademoiselle," he responded, scurrying off to fulfill her request.

Everyone on her house staff was bilingual, and the majority were bisexual as well. Aunt Val liked talented tongues around her, able to communicate in diverse ways.

"Auntie," I said after a pause, "I've been here almost ten minutes, and you've yet to utter a single word about what you're doing currently—what new causes and crusades you're locked into. Don't tell me the well has run dry!"

Her eyes fluttered and her sensuous mouth rippled. "I'm just trying to exercise some control over my emotions," she confessed. "I'm always letting my enthusiasms interfere with my communications with those I love. But of course the well has not run dry—no more than has the well of my womb."

"That's good news," I replied lightly, "because I know that's always at flood stage."

The zealot gleam had already entered her eyes at the mention of her missions. I doubted whether she even heard my last comment.

"It's sweet of you to be concerned with my work," she said in a hushed voice. "It's my reason for being on earth, Nicole. God put me here to help the helpless and inspire the confused."

"He did a very compelling packaging job, too," I noted, striving to keep her from lapsing into evangelistic excess. "You look as though you just won the Miss Teenage Sex Symbol pageant.''

Her eyes misted over.

"God is sex and sex is God," she chanted. "That is my message to convey to the world. Never be ashamed of your body and its appetites, for lust is the most honest of all human emotions."

"Heavy, heavy, Auntie," I responded, rolling back my eyes.

"Your life has been blessed—as has mine—by the capacity to understand and enjoy the luxury of our libidos without the terrifying inhibitions so many others have constraining them," she continued, fervor mounting in her voice. "I am bound by my commitment to the cause of mankind's sexual salvation to carry the various messages and methods of deliverance from sexual slavery to the four corners of the world . . ."

"I understand," I said in a low, barely audible voice. "It's as holy as my hole."

She rose as if on an angelic, spiritual mission, staring ahead. Her arms moved over her head like those of a diver on a high board. She was in one of her ecstatic trances, and I had no choice but to sweat it out until it was over. As usual, though, the wait was considerable. It ended with her collapse in my arms, sobbing for joy. "I'm purified once more!" she declared.

By the time dinner was announced, hours after my arrival, I had still not heard of any new crusade on Aunt Val's part. But that condition was destined to be alleviated shortly after dessert had been served. Good old reliable Auntie was indeed off and running toward a new goal—one which I had inadvertently cooperated in espousing that very afternoon.

"It's a most important cause for civilization,"

she revealed over espresso laced with cognac. "The Universal Sixty-Nine Society."

"*Cunt*gratulations!" I cried, holding my cup aloft.

Aunt Valerie frowned. "I'm serious, child," she declared.

"But of course you are," I agreed. "I think it's a marvelous undertaking."

"Come with me to the slogan room," she invited, rising to take my hand.

"As soon as I finish my espresso." I knew that made her impatient but I was determined to relax before the rigors of reunion. Auntie was such a bundle of energy that she could wear out a kindergarten class, much less a girl who'd been through the acrobatics of hours of sixty-nining and "suffered" the sweet agonies of at least a hundred climaxes. She had been there too, of course, but her resiliency was remarkable.

After I had downed the last drop from my cup, I made a sweeping gesture with my arms.

"Lead me to your lair of liberated licentiousness," I told her.

She glanced at me with a suddenly aloof air of exasperation. When Aunt Valerie was serious about something, it was *de rigueur* that everyone else regard the subject seriously also.

We passed the hive of offices harboring her dedicated drones, all of them so absorbed in whatever they were doing that they never looked up to acknowledge either of us.

"I have a good, devoted crew now," she commented in transit. "They scarcely look at the clock. Sometimes after midnight, when I slip down for a late drink or snack, some of them are still toiling away."

"That's wonderful!" I responded.

"It's such a rewarding feeling. Seeing them

aiding my work reassures me that all the effort is worth it, that all my sacrifices are not in vain."

Sacrifices? I thought to myself. Auntie had no financial worries, no health problems, indulged in any manner and amount of sexual activity that appealed to her, traveled the world freely and fell in and out of love with delicious abandon—enjoying each new romance to the fullest before turning to another.

The slogan room, as she called it, was really the headquarters of her publicity and promotional units. The title came from the cork-lined walls which were studded with neatly and variously printed signs relating to the most current cause being ballyhooed internationally. The name of the *Universal Sixty-Nine Society* left little doubt of its advocacy.

"They've been very clever with this one," she announced with obvious satisfaction. "Just take a look at the wit on the walls."

I moved in closer and let my eyes roam over the pasteboard placards.

"Sixty-Nine is Divine!" proclaimed one.

"Don't Be a Loon—69 Someone Soon!"

They continued along the walls, all along the same lines:

"Follow the Golden Rule: Sixty-Nine!"

"You're the Winner When You're Licked!"

"Cunt is Delicious, Cock is Divine, When You Combine Them in Sixty-Nine!"

"Cunnilingus & Fellatio Go Together Like Alger & Horatio."

"Come Together By Going Down Together!"

"The Meat Is Sweet Where All Legs Meet!"

"Cunt or Cock—It Doesn't Matter, Just Enjoy the Juicy Batter!"

"Put Your Head Between Her Legs While She Sucks Your Hairy Eggs."

"It's Fun to Be a Sucker When the Score is 69!"
"Cock or Cunt Your Problem? Face It, Embrace It. Sixty-Nine!"

I sat down at the edge of one of the desks. "Auntie, this is too much. I think it's a wonderful program. Really inspiring."

She glowed "I'm so glad you approve, Nicole. You're such a marvelously understanding and enthusiastic child."

Later, alone in my room, I laughed and fingered myself, visions of sixes and nines copulating in a numerical orgy inside my head.

chapter four

Gilda joined the madcap menagerie at Aunt Valerie's two days after my arrival, accompanied by a pair of bisexual male ballet dancers named Jorge and José. They entertained us almost immediately with a naked fencing duel, their long, hard cocks serving as their sabers.

"Touché!" rang out repeatedly from the mouths of Gilda, Aunt Val and myself as the bis with a bias for boys pricked each other with their pricks time after time.

Their proud phallic weapons glistened as the mock battle progressed. The winner would be the one who could longest restrain himself from climaxing, the mark of his victory a christening with come from the other.

"Fuck him, José!" Gilda shrieked as he made contact with Jorge's anus.

"Don't come, Jorge!" Aunt Val entered the spirit of things. "Make him pop first!"

It was ludicrous in one sense, but tantalizing in

another. They both were well endowed not only from a penile standpoint, but with pendulous scrotums as well. Just watching their cocks clash while their balls danced was inspired choreography in itself. They heightened the ballet effect from time to time by rising on their tiptoes while flailing and flogging one another's roosterish cocks.

"Hang in there, José!" Gilda shouted, showing her preference once again.

We would have no conflict there. My first and continuing choice between the two was Jorge with his long eyelashes and sensitive, sensual mouth. His flat abdomen was beautifully jeweled by a provocatively intriguing navel that resembled an infant's pussy.

"Hold back, Jorge!" I urged him. "Save it all for me!"

He glanced over at me, his eyes fleetingly amused, his mouth curling into a tight smile. Beads of perspiration decorated his brow as he twisted and turned, arched and lunged, maneuvering his bobbing prick with graceful agility.

"I should endow a Foundation for Phallic Fencing," Aunt Valerie mused. "It's such a healthy, virile, stimulating sport."

"A coming attraction, too," I jibed.

Aunt Val smiled smugly. "That has yet to be proved."

The proof was in the pudding very soon thereafter. Both of the handsome, muscular young men were at the bursting point, the veins of their swollen swords standing out in bas relief. Little pearls of fore-come topped the tips of their cocks, heralding the imminent attack from a navy of semen waiting to charge.

José's face mirrored the strain of delaying orgasm. His brow corrugated, silvered with sweat, and his lips were clenched.

"No, José!" Gilda screamed, sensing defeat.

She was intuitive. A split-second later he moaned in disgust as his prick reared like a wild stallion, spitting globs of eggy come into high arcs that landed in small lakes on the floor and on the heaving, perspiring body of Jorge.

"Vencedor!" Jorge proclaimed himself, holding a clenched fist aloft while the other surrounded the pulsating meat of his prick.

In three quick strokes, he brought himself off, aiming his copious stockpile of sperm at José, splattering him with the seeds of his triumph. José looked defeated but it was all really in fun—and both were victors. They both enjoyed abundant orgasms, and now they had three succulent suckers to lick their wounds and bring them to further climaxes. It evolved into a most entertaining and rewarding afternoon, including some extremely intriguing male-on-male fucking and sucking after we had finished with them temporarily. Aunt Valerie insisted she was serious about her brainstorm, a Foundation for Phallic Fencing, but I became so busy making a heroine sandwich of myself between the buns of Jorge and José I scarcely paid any heed. They were an amusing pair, willing to try anything that promised the potential for popping their pricks.

Later, when I was finally able to converse with Gilda alone, the two of us masturbated one another while we discussed our plans for the reunion.

"Remember Dr. Duncan who taught English literature?" I asked, playing her clit like a tuning fork.

"The one who addressed everybody as 'thee' and 'thou' and all that Elizabethan shit?" Gilda laughed.

"Cute, though?"

"In a professorial way I guess."

"I want to fuck him," I confessed.

"Do it. The guy I'm after is Monsieur Tremain. I always wanted to fuck him and suck his cock."

"God knows you made it obvious enough," I recalled, "spreading your legs in class and sucking your thumb everytime he looked at you."

"He was afraid, I guess. Rules and regulations interfere with so many potentially great lays."

"We never let them stop us often," I reminded her.

"Just most of the fucking faculty, that's all," she complained. "They're always so fearful of their reputations."

"It's not easy getting a teaching job if you're known as a student fucker."

I quickly spun about so that I was facing her dark-haired pussy and lowered my own onto her poised and waiting lips. Swiftly and silently we returned to being classmates and assmates in the truest and most rewarding sense. Our reunion had begun even before it began formally and in the best way possible: sharing orgasms between the Académie Dumont's two dearest friends and undoubtedly its most actively amorous alumnae.

chapter five

With José and Jorge dispatched back to Rio and with Aunt Valerie immersed in her *Universal Sixty-Nine Society* and the fledgling *Foundation for Phallic Fencing*, it seemed an opportune time for Gilda and me to escape to Count Erich's pink marble chateau on the outskirts of Paris near the Académie Dumont. I utilized it seldom despite its convenience because when I was away from the castle I preferred to be spontaneous, and if necessary secretive, about my movements, involvements, and activities. This time, however, both the count and countess were well aware of where I was at and for what occasion, so it hardly mattered.

Arriving at the gates, I was struck again by the beauty of the place and the meticulous gardens surrounding it. I really would have to take advantage of its availability more often in the future, I told myself. As for Gilda, she slept through the drive despite the fact I had borrowed Auntie's new Lamborghini Countach and floored the accelerator for several stretches of temptingly open high-way.

"Wake up!" I said, prodding her in the rib cage with my index finger. "You've arrived at the pearly gates."

She stirred and rubbed her eyes, yawning and stretching sensually. "Wrong place," she muttered. "I go to the one with flames licking at your feet."

"Even the fires of hell would know there's a better place to lick on you than your feet!"

"I must have konked out!"

"At 180 kilometers an hour that's some feat."

"Back to feet again?" she questioned.

"Go suck your toes!" I exclaimed, sliding out of the driver's seat. "I'm going in to announce our presence to the housekeeper."

"Don't abandon me," she responded, jumping out of the car. "I'm alive and well and living in Paris—just like Jacques Brel."

"Jockstrap," I jested.

"Balls," she protested, slapping my rump as she scrambled to keep up with me.

"Behave yourself," I instructed her. "These are gentle old people who take care of the place for Count Erich."

"I can be a lady when I want to!"

"You can be laid when you want to, too," I retorted.

"Playing with words again," she sighed.

"Go play with yourself!" I shot back, adding immediately, "Sssssshhhh."

We were at the door with its gleaming brass knob and knocker. I tapped it gently—one, two, three times. There was a moment's hesitation and then it swung open, revealing not a little old man or lady, but a coltish young woman with breasts poking provocatively outward from a cotton T-shirt. She looked about eighteen.

"What's happened to Madame Dusha.?" I asked in surprise.

"She's in the city."

"And Monsieur Dushay?"

"He went for fertilizer at the market."

Both Gilda and I were intrigued by the physical attractiveness and freshness of the young lady. I knew that from an exchange of glances between us.

"Are you working here, too?" I ventured to ask.

"No, I'm visiting grandmother and grandpa."

"May we come in?" Gilda asked.

She seemed reluctant. "Grandpa said not to let anybody in," she related.

"I'm Nicole," I explained. "Count Erich sent me."

"It's perfectly all right," Gilda assured her. "Nicole is like a daughter to the count and countess."

The young woman looked us over without embarrassment.

"What's your name?" I inquired.

"Lysange."

"That's pretty. Lysange, this is Gilda."

"Hi."

"Hi."

"Do you think you might let us in now?" I asked.

She still was hesitant, her eyes searching the road behind us. It was easy to understand why Paul Dushay did not want his granddaughter admitting just any old stranger. She was a tempting creature.

"Here comes grandpa!" she announced with obvious relief. The decision to admit us now would not have to be hers to make.

"Paul!" I shouted to him as he drove up in the small pickup truck he used for carting tools and supplies.

"Nicole!" he reacted with genuine delight.

Lysange looked pleased and relieved as we embraced.

"I think your granddaughter was dubious about letting us in," I whispered to him.

"I should have remembered that you were due any day," he apologized. "Otherwise I tell her never to admit anyone on any pretense whatever."

"I can understand that," I said. "She's very pretty."

"As you well know, the world's full of lechers," he remarked with a twinkle in his eyes.

"This is my dear friend Gilda," I finally remembered to say. "Paul Dushay."

"Hello, Paul," Gilda responded with a warm smile.

"My pleasure, Gilda. If you're a friend of Nicole's, you're definitely a friend of the Dushays."

Lysange was now as warm and friendly as she had been wary and aloof earlier. "I like you," she whispered, offering her lips for a kiss.

I swept my mouth over hers. "Sleep with me tonight."

"Really?"

"Really." I assured her.

Her fawn's eyes sparkled. "Leave the door unlocked," she whispered. "I'll come to you after grandmother and grandpa are asleep."

With that as a promise, I had ample reason to look forward to nightfall.

Brigitte Dushay returned from shopping all aflutter over our presence. "The house is a mess," she lamented. "If I'd known you were coming so soon, I'd have stayed to put it in order."

"It's impeccable as always, Brigitte," I assured her. "You have no reason to apologize."

"Oh, dear," she sighed, hands pulling at her cheeks. "Nicole, I'm sorry. The count and countess would never forgive me."

"Nonsense! When I speak to them tonight, I'm going to tell them the truth—the chateau is immaculate."

"Listen to her, Mama," her husband advised. "She wouldn't lie to you."

"I'd eat off the floors," Gilda commented.

I glanced at her with a *double entendre* in mind, but decided it would be inappropriate.

"Brigitte, this is my good friend and Académie Dumont classmate, Gilda Morrow," I said.

Brigitte curtsied as though in the presence of royalty. "Pleased to meet you, mademoiselle," she responded.

"It's my pleasure to meet you, Madame Dushay," Gilda replied.

"Gilda and Brigitte," I insisted. "I like everybody to be on a first-name basis."

"You learned that in America," Paul observed.

"Yes, and it's much, much friendlier."

"It does make verbal intercourse easier," Gilda said.

"And sexual, too," I was compelled to note.

Brigitte blushed, Paul cleared his throat, and Lysange tittered. Gilda and I merely smiled at one another over the obvious setup between us.

"I'll show you to your rooms," Brigitte said when she had recovered sufficiently from her embarrassment. "I do hope they're in better condition than the main floor."

"Brig-it-ttttte," I dragged out her name in reproach.

"I'll do it, Grandma," Lysange volunteered.

Brigitte looked surprised by her granddaughter's offer.

"You? Helping grandma without being asked?"

"I know where everything is."

"Go ahead, then," Brigitte waved her off. "It'll give me a chance to get some canapés ready. I'm sure Nicole and Gilda would like a few welcoming cocktails."

"That would be nice," I agreed.

"Come," Lysange beckoned.

I could come just looking at you, I thought to myself. Her tits jiggled enticingly behind her skimpy shirt and as she ascended the broad staircase ahead of us her ass was absolutely bewitching in its undulations.

"We're right behind your beautiful behind," I told her, low enough so that neither Dushay could hear me.

"Isn't it a work of art?" Gilda agreed.

Lysange peered over her shoulder, puckered, and pretended to throw us both a kiss.

I couldn't resist feeling her rump the moment we were out of sight of the caretakers. Instead of shying away, Lysange backed firmly into my clutch.

"Playing grab-ass, huh?" Gilda observed. "I know that game, too."

With that she filled her palm with a handful of firm, tender derrière, meeting my fingers in the crack between Lysange's cheeks. It was only a matter of moments before each of us had our free hand cupping one of her breasts as well.

"Ooooh!" Lysange gasped, surprised by our instant aggressiveness.

"Where are the rooms, honey?" I asked with a sense of urgency.

She nodded with her head, indicating a doorway to the right. Quickly Gilda and I spirited her into the first suite and flung her to the bed. My blood was racing, and I was sure Gilda's was as well. The jeans came off like the peel of a banana, and the shirt slid over her shoulders and head in one swift movement. All at once she was there before us, succulently naked.

"What—?" she uttered before Gilda sealed her mouth with a torrid kiss.

I separated her legs and dove face-first into the dewy pink configuration of her cunt, my tongue racing ahead of the rest of my face. Gilda had already mounted and straddled her, feeding her sable pussy to the mouth she had been kissing only moments before. Neither of us knew for certain that Lysange was cunnilingual, but we were determined to teach her this marvelous language of love.

"Suck it, sweetheart," Gilda encouraged her, and, indirectly, me.

Lysange wriggled and rose and pitched to and fro like a cork in the sea as my mouth organ played hot licks on her clitoris. Abruptly, her back arched and the mound of her pussy pressed with tremendous passion against my face. She was coming—and coming furiously—the awareness of which required only one flick of my finger on my own clit to sink me into the delicious depths of orgasm.

"Cunt suck, fuck, shit!" Gilda screeched, a sure sign she was also in the throes of climax.

I watched her asshole twitch as she exploded just above me. The sparse fuzz of Lysange's young crack afforded me a clear view of Gilda's gorgeous buttocks. In the grip of orgasm, they seemed even more appealing than ever.

"Lysange!" the unmistakable voice of Madame

Dushay echoed through the corridor.

Never did such a trio of ardent amorists lock up their lusts so instantly as did we at the sound of the call. Frantically we restored Lysange to her prior clothed state, but not without difficulty. The feverish oral fucking had left us all bathed in perspiration, and that in turn made it difficult to pull on her tight jeans and force down her T-shirt over her wet chest.

"Yes, Grandmother?" the girl responded, fear replacing passion in her eyes.

"Why is it taking you so long? I have the cocktails and canapés ready for our guests."

"We'll be there momentarily, Brigitte," I replied, taking over for her granddaughter.

"Whenever you're ready," Brigitte called, although her tone implied no such leeway.

"Whew!" Lysange sighed, feigning wiping her brow in relief.

"You are delectable," Gilda whispered to her, feeling her as she spoke.

"I'm the one who ate her," I pointed out.

"One does not have to dine to recognize that an entrée is delicious," she retorted. "You should be grateful I let you be first."

Lysange seemed slightly shy now that she was clothed again.

"How did you like it, darling?" I questioned her.

"It was my very first time," she confessed.

"You mean with girls?"

"With anybody."

"My God!" Gilda exclaimed. "I didn't know there were any virgins left!"

"No wonder the flavor was beyond description," I said, patting her soft, dark hair.

"I will come to you tonight," Lysange promised.

"You did like it then?" I asked, peering into her lively dark eyes.

"It was more wonderful than even my wildest dreams," she said.

"We'll do our best to make it even better tonight," Gilda pledged.

With that as a shared promise, the three of us descended the staircase, looking as subdued and innocent as a trio of Vestal Virgins.

chapter six

What a lyrical night it had been! The delightfully devilish and carnally clever Lysange squirmed and giggled between us, licking and laughing, fingering and frolicking like an exuberant youngster in the Bois de Boulogne. At that, her cunt was like cotton candy, pink as a sunrise, her tits as lickable as candied apples. Her virgin fantasies had worked remarkably well to inspire her premiere performances in the calisthenics of cunnilingus. She sucked like a sibling of Sappho from the beginning, and her digits were dexterous substitutes for cocks and tongues inside our willing wombs.

But the marble chateau was meant to be only a brief stopover en route to the Académie and the reunion. I knew by Lysange's sullen expression that she did not like my breakfast announcement that Gilda and I would be leaving for the Dumont campus sometime that afternoon.

"But you only just got here!" she protested

despite a chilling look from Brigitte.

"Lysange," her grandmother chided her, "we are here for the convenience and accommodation of the count's guests—not to pass judgment on their schedules."

"She is a darling to be concerned," I said with sincerity. "Both Gilda and I have been so impressed in such a brief time with her loveliness and maturity."

"Absolutely," Gilda confirmed. "If she were at Dumont, she'd be president of her class for certain."

"I only wish that we could afford such a fine education for her," Paul Dushay commented. "Look what it's done for you two young ladies."

"We did learn a lot there," I agreed, smiling at Gilda.

"I think Lysange could go directly into an advanced class," Gilda suggested.

Nothing we said made the sparkle return to Lysange's dramatic eyes. She was visibly upset over the immediacy of our departure.

"Eat your sausages, child," her grandmother urged her.

"Nicole and Gilda have champagne and berries," she complained.

"Have some too, then," Brigitte said.

"No," Lysange snapped. "I'm not at all hungry for anything—or anyone—at this table."

Paul Dushay put his napkin on the table and stared at her. "That is an odd remark," he said.

"It's nothing," I injected quickly. "I feel dreadful myself about leaving so soon, especially after meeting your marvelous granddaughter. We would love to spend more time."

Gilda came to my aid. "Had we known it, we could have shortened our visit with Nicole's Aunt Valerie."

"She's my pet cuckoo bird," I explained with a chuckle.

"I believe we met her once, Nicole," Brigitte said. "She was promoting villas in a nudist colony, if I recall correctly."

"That sounds like her," I laughed.

"The one and only," Gilda agreed.

Lysange excused herself, tears in her eyes, and fled upstairs.

"I feel dreadful about making her so upset," I confessed.

Brigitte dismissed the scene. "She's impressionable. I guess it's boring for her to be around two old people all the time."

"There are young people her own age down the road," Paul reminded his wife. "It's just that she dreams of being like Gilda and Nicole—beautiful and sophisticated."

I went upstairs to console Lysange. I'd already made up my mind to present her with the platinum vibrator Peter Theophilus had given me a year ago. It proved to be just the right gift to uplift her mood.

"Every time I come, I'll think of you," she said.

"That is a lovely tribute, Lysange," I replied, kissing the top of her head.

"You will come back soon, won't you?" she inquired.

"Absolutely. Maybe even right after the reunion."

"How long is that?" she asked eagerly.

"A week."

Her eyes recovered their luster. "It'll seem like forever, but I know it'll just be seven days."

We kissed and I felt once again the warm, moist jewel of her loins. Our sexing undoubtedly would have gone farther if Gilda and Brigitte hadn't walked in.

"My, my," Brigitte noted, "our gloomy young lady is actually smiling."

"I promised we'd stop back after the reunion," I explained.

"Good idea," Gilda seconded the motion.

Brigitte clapped her hands. "This time the chateau will be in proper order."

In that climate of restored happiness, Gilda and I packed to move on. Registration was due to begin at the Académie immediately after lunch. I think we both felt just slightly nervous and apprehensive at the thought of it. But it was the good kind of butterflies—those that promised a memorable week of merrymaking. By noon we were back in the Lamborghini, fluttering waves to Paul, Brigitte and Lysange before roaring off into the French countryside.

Returning to Dumont was a revelation of sorts. Even with the perspective of only a few years, everything about the campus and buildings had become miniaturized. The great halls of the administration building now looked more like the narrow corridors of an urban hotel. The once-majestic steeple of the chapel seemed more like an enlarged vaccination needle than an inspiring spire spearing the sky. In fact, physically, the whole of it was diminished in my eyes—far less formidable and imposing than I remembered it as a student.

Gilda shared my initial disillusionment. "Doesn't seem the same, does it?" she asked after our quickie survey of the mostly deserted halls and grounds.

"No," I admitted, "but then we're earlybirds. Wait till everybody's here and then see what it's like."

"Nothing's ever the same when you return after a long absence. We've been all over the world since we last skipped around these paths."

"Sad in a way, isn't it?" I sighed.

"Think of how it'll be fifty years from now."

"Fifty years?" I exclaimed. "I'll be dead for thirty by that time."

Gilda laughed. "Everybody figures on dying young—when they're young. It's a different story when they get older."

"How would you know?" I questioned.

"My mother told me that a long time ago."

"Do you believe it?"

"I'll let you know when I'm older."

"Drop a note in my crypt."

"Jesus, Nicole, yesterday you were all hyped up about coming back here. Now you're Miss Melancholy."

"I don't know what I expected, but I do feel let down."

"Give the damned thing a chance, will you? We just got here. We're not even signed in yet!"

"I'm sorry," I apologized. "Let's register."

The gym was reunion headquarters, with long tables bearing various letters of the alphabet. It was festooned with balloons and bunting, the sight of which immediately buoyed my spirits. At least it was beginning to look a bit more like a celebration than a wake.

"I'll bet you they have me under the 'L's' instead of the 'N's'," I predicted.

"You hate that, don't you?"

"I just want to be known as Nicole, damn it, and nobody seems to want to allow me to have it my way."

"Dr. Beauregard is a stickler for propriety, remember?"

"Except when he's entertaining female faculty in his quarters!"

"Those are just rumors, Nicole."

"Remember that picture somebody made up

and circulated, showing the headmaster giving head to one of the English teachers?'' I recalled with amusement.

"It got two students banished, didn't it?"

"The wrong ones, too. I know who did it—and she graduated with honors."

"In photography?" Gilda joked.

"In pornography."

Somehow in the ensuing moments as we stood poised to enter the auditorium/gymnasium, it became increasingly alive with people, many of their faces familiar even though their names did not come immediately to mind. The surge of celebrants sent my spirits up another notch.

"It's building," I observed to Gilda.

"Let's go in and see who's here," she suggested.

Hand-in-hand, as we had gone about the campus so often in years past, Gilda and I made our entry into the now-bustling arena.

"Nicole!" someone shrieked.

"Gilda!" screamed another.

We were quickly surrounded by a small covey of yelling, grasping former classmates, smiling and grinning, throwing kisses and waving banners, mimicking the scene of an athletic rally.

"You're here, you dolls!" sang out our most alluring former rival, Cody Cameron.

"Cody!" I cried out in response, waving frantically.

A tall fellow whom I recalled only vaguely pinned back my arm and proceeded to plant an intimate kiss on my lips.

"Welcome," he said when he finally broke the seal.

"Thanks, I think," I replied dazedly.

Gilda was all aflutter, kissing men and women alike as they passed by in an impromptu receiving line of graduates and guests.

"Which one of you was The Girl Most Likely to Suck?" a dashing Eric Blye inquired aloud. Throughout our last year, Cody had kept his picture on her bed, of all places.

"It doesn't matter," Gilda answered him. "We're now joint holders of the title."

Self-conscious but nonetheless uproarious laughter greeted her response. Forgotten now was my earlier disappointment. Reunion fever had set in and I was ready—wow, was I ready!—to pull out all stops and open all orifices. "Do Your Thing at Dumont!" one of the banners proclaimed. Indeed I would—in my own highly inimitable fashion—no holes barred.

chapter seven

Académie Dumont was rife with revelry from the moment our presence permeated the campus. Whether it was the musk of our muffs, the jiggle of our jugs or the lust of our laughter—both Gilda and I seemed to possess some catalytic quality that was *cunt*agious and *prick*ceptive at the same time. It was Mardi Gras and New Year's Eve and the beginning of World War III all together from the instant we scratched our names onto the registration ledgers—mine thankfully on the table next to hers under 'N' to my delighted surprise—and we did nothing to discourage the regal regard in which we seemed to be held by student body and faculty alike.

"Ni-cole! Ni-cole! Ni-cole!" a random cheering section took up the chant, varying it alternately with "Gil-da! Gil-da! Gil-da!"

It was warm enough to bring tears to my eyes and Gilda, ever the follower and close runner-up, soon had glistening jewels in the corners of each of her lovely orbs as well.

There was so much milling about, so much tugging and shouting, that it took me some time before I was able to spot dear pipe-smoking Dr. Duncan, a book as always clutched in his armpit, standing off quietly surveying the mounting pandemonium. Graduates from all over the globe—ten years' worth of alumnae—were congregating to celebrate "A Decade of Dumont." How could I ever have doubted it would eventually materialize into something as wild and wonderful as this?

"I'm going over to say hello to Dr. Duncan," I said breathlessly to Gilda.

"Look for Monsieur Tremain for me," she pleaded, wriggling from the too-intimate chest grasp of an older graduate's guest whom I'd never seen before.

"I will," I promised.

As I forded the tide of bodies, my own was goosed and grabbed repeatedly by eager-eyed young men and, encouragingly, several cute former classmates. There would definitely be no shortage of fertile flesh for laying in the week that lay ahead.

"Dr. Duncan! Dr. Duncan!" I waved and called out as I neared him.

He looked about vaguely, bemused in the midst of bedlam. Perhaps he wouldn't even remember me, I thought with sudden anxiety. I had more or less always assumed that anyone I remembered must certainly remember me. What if that were not true of men like the good Dr. Duncan—men to whom the past held more allure than either the present or the future? But I should not have agonized over it even fleetingly; the moment he became aware of me, his angular figure and aesthetic, sensitive face became more animated than I could recall ever having seen it before.

"Nicole!" he greeted me warmly, arms outstretched to embrace me. "Dear child, how nice it is to see thee again."

I fell into his arms as naturally as if he were my father. Perhaps that was what he represented to me—a youngish father figure. I had never thought of it that way until the moment I felt his arms tighten about me. It was good then that I had a keen sense of family because I had always felt a special erotic attraction to his man who taught English literature in speech flavored with Elizabethan terms.

"Oh, Dr. Duncan, how I miss your classes!" I confessed. "You'll never believe it, but I can still recite from Chaucer's *Legend of Good Women* after all this time."

"Dear Geoffrey?" he responded with a pleased expression. "I'm not surprised at your scholarship, for thine is a special gift of beauty and intelligence. Prithee, tell me what thou hast been doing, lo, these many days and nights past since departing Dumont."

"Running," I replied candidly. "Dashing all over the world in pursuit of entertainment and excitement."

"Thou hast returned it to the Académie this day. Cast thine eyes on the bedlam."

"I'd rather cast my thighs on the bed."

"Ever the wit, dearest Nicole. Thy presence was akin to having the moon and the stars as my pupils."

"My pupils are more like amethysts, I'm told." I peered into his soft brown eyes.

"Violaceous they are indeed. How unique and compelling."

"You never noticed them before, Doctor?" I asked, breathing against his face.

"Thou must be forgiving, Nicole, for I am the victim of myopia."

"And mythology?"

He smiled faintly. "Yes, the latter by choice."

"You may be nearsighted, Doctor, but you're very farsighted in your teaching."

"How kind of thee. The love of literature is germane to the soul."

"And the love of erotic literature?" I teased, feeling remarkably comfortable with him now that I was an alumna.

"Germane to the libido," he replied with another small smile.

Gilda apparently could not tolerate such immediate student/faculty closeness, especially in the absence of her pet pedagogue, Monsieur Tremain. She shook off the covey of admirers surrounding her and approached us with swift, positive strides.

"This place is a madhouse," she protested to me. "Let's get out of here for a while and just look around."

"Don't you speak to Dr. Duncan?" I asked in response.

"I never took English lit, but hi, anyway, Dr. D."

Roderick was mildly taken aback by her flippancy, but he took it more or less in stride.

"Thou art a lovely representative of Dumont to the world at large. Gilda Morrow. Prithee, am I correct?"

"The privy is down the hallway, Doc," she retorted with shocking gaucherie. "You've been here long enough to know that by now."

"Thou art in the Boswell tradition," Dr. Duncan said with no air of dismay or condescension. In fact, he seemed wryly amused.

"Gilda!" I reprimanded her with only the enunciation of her name. I knew her well enough to know that she was reacting out of jealousy over my immediate first step toward fulfillment of the fantasies we'd discussed. She could be *so* impatient! And so envious.

"Are you coming with me or coming with him?" she demanded.

Another gaffe with a gaff, *double entendre*.

"I'll catch up with you in a minute or two," I promised. "Meet me by the wishing well."

"Don't tempt me to make a nasty wish," she retorted.

"The mood you're in, that's the only kind you could make!"

Gilda spun on her spiked heel and strode off without another word.

"Impetuous, wouldst thou not say, fair maiden?" Dr. Duncan observed with an air of curiosity.

"Damn her!" I muttered, furious over her brief tantrum.

"Beautiful lasses oft have clashes," he recited as though quoting from somewhere.

"Shakespeare?" I asked.

"No," he replied coyly. "A Duncan *bon mot.*"

"That's better than a Duncan donut," I parried.

"That's dubious," he replied.

"Dubious Duncan. I always wondered whether you had a first name, Doctor."

"That's obvious—but it's not Dubious." He displayed some of the classroom kittenishness which had endeared him to many of his students, but perhaps to none more than me.

"Just for the spell of it, what would it be?"

"Roderick," he confessed.

"You're a Rod!"

"But I don't spare myself, lest I spoil the child."

"Yeah, though I walk through the valley of the shadow of death, my Rod and his staff shall comfort me," I proclaimed in jest.

"Thou art marvelously alert and alive."

"Come with me to find Gilda."

"Would that I could, but I am by dint of decree of Dr. Marcel Beauregard assigned to the faculty committee overseeing the reunion. I must therefore remain where I am until registration ceases for the day, only to resume on the morrow."

"That leaves you free tonight?"

"Poetically licensed."

"And licentiously?" I felt bold enough to ask.

"Erotically licensed."

I squeezed his hand and he lifted mine and opened it like a flower. Then, to my surprise, he tickled the palm of it—an ancient erotic rite.

"I'll be in the library doing research from seven P.M. until perhaps ten or ten-thirty," he disclosed.

"Look for me in Row N of the classics," I told him. "The 'N' is for two words—Nicole and naughty."

"That is most alliteratively alluring. Bearing that in mind, I shall confine my evening's probings to Friedrich Nietzsche."

"I hope in your probings of Nicole you will bare more than your mind," I quipped.

"Verily," he promised with a smile, kissing my open hand.

I tripped off to find Gilda, hardly noticing all the activity around me. It was only the eve of the reunion, and already I was headlong into my most prized fantasy of the week. It was a good omen for a good orgasm, so I sidetracked to the ladies' room to achieve it. The great god of onanism was never more generous to me. By the time I found Gilda, I had tiptoed through the two lips of my twat so successfully I was as giddy as if I'd taken white lady along. And the day had really just begun.

chapter eight

Inside the library, with its floor-to-ceiling shelves
of books creating a literary labyrinth, the atmosphere was in marked contrast to the increasingly
raucous revelry on the school grounds. Everyone
seemed to be wandering about with bottles of
champagne clutched in their fists, drinking and
carousing in the very places they once trod in
uniforms under strict regulations. There was a
sense of triumph in the act of flouting the
academic disciplines openly where once we had
done so covertly. But now, in the library, the
climate was again—or rather still—scholastic.

I felt just a shade out of uniform in my spike-
heeled shoes, miniskirt, and tight-fitting tank top.
The librarian, in stereotypical horn-rimmed
glasses, peered at me just long enough to convey
her distaste for my apparel and perhaps my
presence as well. Gratefully, from my standpoint,
she disappeared quickly into a huge volume before
her on the desk, leaving only her fingers visible as

they held the outer edges.

The room was huge and deserted, with seemingly everyone on campus engaged in celebrating the eve of reunion week. Everyone—that is—except a certain amorous alumna named Nicole and a certain sly instructor of English literature named Dr. Roderick Duncan. At least I hoped and expected he was there. Glancing about I saw no immediate sign of him, and I had no desire to enlist the librarian in a search for him lest she draw the wrong—though really the right—conclusion.

I made a pretense of looking up something in the Dewey Decimal System files, wisely pulling out one of the "N" drawers and leaving it that way when I left. Librarians were notoriously curious creatures, so I wanted to be sure any encounter with Dr. Duncan would appear to be coincidental.

The walls of books were like corridors in a high-ceilinged castle, their bulk serving as very effective soundproofing and insulation from the central area of the library. However, my heels did click audibly as I made my way across the polished floor to the mid-alphabet rows. Click-click, suck-a-dick, I accompanied the sounds mentally.

Since the rows fanned out from the hub of the room, they were long enough to require several intersecting breaks from one to another. I found Dr. Duncan there in one of the hidden crossover passages between "N" and "O."

"You're spelling NO even before we've begun," I whispered behind him. He lurched, startled, almost dropping the open book in his hands.

"Thou dost taketh a scholar by surprise, my dear."

"We seem to be the only two people in here, not counting Miss Prissy, the librarian."

"Edith Gallenzar," he corrected.

"Is she nosy?"

"Not if we're not noisy."

"The quietest activities in the world are fellatio and cunnilingus," I declared.

"Nicole! Those words are not even in most standard dictionaries."

"Suck, then. That's in all of them."

"With quite a different connotation," he insisted.

"To suck is to draw into the mouth by forming a partial vacuum with the lips and tongue," I recited as if by rote.

He looked at me with faint amusement. "I do believe that thou hast orated a reasonably lexicographical definition of the verb sucketh."

"Orally?" I responded with a Tallulah Bankhead-ish twang.

"Thou hast a splendid head on thy shoulders." He touched me for the first time, a bit tentatively, on the nape of my neck. It sent a ripple of excitement surfing through my anatomy.

"Speaking of head," I said, then stopped. I doubted whether Dr. Duncan was aware of such jazzy jargon, especially on such a juicy subject. "What's that you're reading?" I changed the subject.

"Thus Spake Zarathustra by Nietzsche. The man was insane—but interesting."

"You're not insane and you're *very* interesting," I said, batting my eyes and pushing out my tits.

"Nicole," he declared intently, "thou art the epitome of erotic temptation without resorting to coquetry. Wouldst thou please abstain?"

"I didn't think you even noticed me," I countered.

"Whether thou believest or not, I am the

57

possessor of an advanced degree in carnal knowledge. And I am an avid student of crotch culture.''

That was all the invitation I needed. Without further ado, I grabbed him at the intersection of his legs and found an encouragingly stiff prick awaiting escape. Swiftly, as he scrutinized me with pipe in hand, I fished out his crimson cock. Freed of its fabric fortress, Rod's rod possessed a commanding presence all its own.

"Here's a live definition of the verb 'suck,' " I declared with a final upward sweep of my gaze before going ahead with my demonstration.

"Tenure be damned!'' he muttered. "Sucketh away, my darling sybarite!''

The tip of his cock was hard and rounded and smooth like the head of a ballpeen hammer. I slid my lips over it like a soft beret, my tongue an inside-out tassel to tickle his tool. His academic reserve evaporated as I proved I was at the head of my class in giving head.

"Oh, William Makepeace Thackerary!'' he groaned with delight. "What a piece I make tonight!''

"Dr. Duncan,'' the voice of the librarian echoed down the aisle, "may I be of any assistance to you?''

Since we were between rows, she could not see us as long as she stayed where she was.

"*Merci*, Mademoiselle Gallenzar,'' Roderick replied in a calm, professorial voice, "but I am quite well off in the hands of the gods and goddesses like Eros and Aphrodite.''

She hesitated momentarily and I waited, both hands clutching the shaft of his organ while my mouth held a solid seal on its crown.

"Do let me know if I can be of help,'' she said, retreating finally.

Dr. Duncan touched the top of my head, his signal to resume. He was as hard as his voice was soft. "Sucketh away, dearest descendant of Venus," he urged.

I had him on the verge of climax several times, the eggs of his scrotum clinging tautly to the base of his prick. Each time I slowed my savage sucking to lengthen the feast for both of us. But now the inquisitiveness of the librarian dictated an early detonation to avoid discovery. I brought him again to the brink—and then over.

"Aughhh!" he cried out involuntarily as a glut of come surged from the head of his swollen cock. I caught most of it in the well of my eager mouth, but it was so abundant that a portion splashed over my face and dripped to the glossy floor.

"What can we use to wipe this up?" I asked hastily, sure she would return to investigate the doctor's audible gasp.

"I have a handkerchief," he said, pulling it from a back pocket and handing it to me.

I blotted away the semen, then fled several rows over when the librarian's footsteps sounded in our direction. Sure enough, she did report to find out the nature of the disturbance.

"Are you sure you're all right, Dr. Duncan?" she demanded now in a direct confrontation.

"I've never been better, thank you," he responded with typical aplomb. "Never ever, Mademoiselle Gallenzar."

I chuckled and fled several rows farther, positioning myself near the exit. It was best that I disappeared while she was talking to Dr. Duncan. I could wait for him outside.

"Where the hell have you been all night?" Gilda demanded from the darkness.

"Gilda? I was doing research."

"Bullshit! You wouldn't go in a library on a

night like this if they were showing color slides of Dr. Duncan's dick.''

"How did you know that was tonight's program?" I teased.

But a moment later the joke backfired when Dr. Duncan emerged from the building, glanced about furtively, and headed for where I was standing.

"Why, you sneaky little bitch!" Gilda railed.

She slipped behind a tree and disappeared into a crowd of chanting grads. God, she could be vile and vicious at times. I shrugged it off this time, however, attributing it to a surfeit of champagne and a mild case of green monster-ism. My blood was still carbonated from hot come and the passion it produced. I wanted my legs to provide an open book for Dr. Duncan's scholarly probing, and apparently he was of the same mind.

"Let us proceed thither to the botanical gardens," he suggested with suave sensuality, "there to continue the original source research begun so admirably in the library."

"Spoken like a biologist," I replied approvingly.

We scurried down a back path to avoid the mainstream of revelers snake-dancing about the lighted parts of the campus. Dr. Duncan surprised me with his knowledge of offbeat paths and cozy clearings I had utilized myself for trysts while a senior. He was not all Shakespeare and Hardy, Wordsworth, and Keats, after all. I considered it a most delightful development.

"Thou wast most marvelous in the library," Roderick remembered to say as we arrived at the gardens. "My gratitude knoweth no bounds."

"I hope your inhibitions are equally boundless," I replied.

"Beauty is in the thighs of the beholder," he

declared, taking out his revitalized rod and aiming it directly at me.

"That's a beauty, all right. And I want it right between my thighs."

"It fucketh with joy," he said, waving it like a scepter.

"Let it fucketh Nicole now," I proposed, lowering myself to a lush green patch of grass shielded by forsythia bushes.

"Shall we risk total nakedness?" he asked, his cock looming like a jet in the sky above me.

"It's the only true way to fuck."

He watched me avidly as I stripped, peeling off his own clothes simultaneously. "If Beauregard ever sees me like this, he'll have no regard for my future at Dumont."

"Beauregard be damned!" I declared, spreading my legs into a seductively lazy yawn. "Let's fuck, dear doctor."

His fat prick lathed into the labyrinth of my cunt as though it had been machine-made for my meat.

"How lyrical," he rhapsodized. "Thine vulva is as beautiful as a verse from Keats or a sonnet from Shakespeare."

"Shake *your* spear in it," I urged him. "Fuck the Dickens out of me!"

"A tail of two titties," he punned.

"I have great expectations," I prolonged the literary parrying. "I expect hard times from our mutual friend."

"Excellent assimilation," he praised me.

"Excellent ass," I replied.

"Superb!" he escalated the adjective.

It was strange and esoteric the way professor and past pupil shared this erotic fusion of education and copulation. The more I thought and shared intellectually with my former teacher, the hotter I got. I was actually several inches off the ground, rooted by feet and hands, desperate to meet the thrusts of his reaming rod.

"Rod, Rod!" I cried. "Oh, my God!"

It was just the first climax of many to come but it shook me like an explosion. My wrists and ankles collapsed under the impact. Roderick rolled me over quickly and began injecting me from the rear, his hands cupping the cheeks of my derrière.

"Fuck me!" I squealed. "Fuck me! Fuck me! Fuck me!"

He was silent now, except for staccato gasps, intent on pleasing himself as well as me. Deeply and deliberately, he rocked in and out of the cradle of my cunt, the friction setting the tissues of my twat aflame. I came again and again, expectant now of his own eggy resolution.

"The cock croweth!" he proclaimed seconds later.

"Ohhhh-ahhhh-ohhhh!" I moaned as the rush of come overflowed the dam of my beaver.

"Cunt of cunts, lord of lords!" he cried out before diving into the soft diamond formed by the meeting of ass and pussy when approached from the rear. His face wedged into the succulent orifice, glued there by the sweet mucilage of mutual lovemaking.

"Leave some of yourself inside me," I pleaded as he sucked away at the liqueur of labia and lob combined in the cavern of my crotch.

I came breathtakingly at the touch of his tongue and the thought of its encounter with the come of his cock inside me. Later when he had surfeited himself with the juices of jism and pussy, I licked his limp and luscious prick clean—and back into a state of rigidity that required us to fuck once again.

It was near midnight when we finally dressed and called it a night. After all, Dr. Duncan was on the faculty reunion committee and would have to be at the gym by seven A.M.

"Will you be all right?" I asked him in parting.

"Thou hast ensured that," he smiled. "I shall be glorious!"

To that I could only add "Amen!" and come tomorrow, the promise to come and come again.

chapter nine

Golden Gilda, sable-cunted and emerald-eyed, wild as war and passionate as the music of Prokofiev, licked her way back into my good graces the morning after the night before.

"I was smashed," she apologized after her tongue-lashing had thrilled me into a full awakening. "Blitzed. Zonked. Shot down."

"Talk to me with your tongue against my clit," I said, languishing lazily in the aftermath of a domino-effect row of climaxes.

"Not until you say I'm forgiven."

"Don't be silly," I sighed. "We've had much more major disputes than that without requiring a peace treaty."

"If you want another piece of my tongue, baby, you'll accept my apology and grant me a pardon."

"I'm granting you a hard-on," I quipped. "My little boy is as stiff as a prick."

"Don't be a shit, Nicole, just say it."

"Suck it," I enunciated with delicious crispness. "Friends are meant to fight and fuck."

"I take the use of the word 'friends' to mean that you've forgiven me," she said, poised now to return to the middle of my muff.

"Breakfast is being served in the parlor of my pussy," I announced as I squirmed.

"I'll be there lickety-split."

"Lick my split, darling," I urged her.

She entered the cave of my cunt like a sensual speleologist, her tongue exploring the slick terrain with the expertise of excellent experience.

"I want you to fuck René Tremain today," I told her with an erotic edge to my voice. "Suck him and fuck him, the bastard sonofabitch!"

We were both word-triggered individuals, inspired to summits of passion by attainable fantasies and bawdy language. My suggestion of seduction of her favorite instructor had the effect that Roderick Duncan did on me. Her tongue turned into a machine for inspired cunt-drilling.

"Chrissakes, Gilda!" I cried out, "you're blowing my fucking fuses!"

The lights did flicker inside my head as a psychedelic display accompanied the outburts of orgasms occurring at my crotch and spreading like wildfire through my body. She threw herself atop me in the midst of the climaxes, sucking my tender, taut nipples even after the major comes had ended.

"What a sweet suck," I purred, keeping my eyes shut to contain the effect.

Naturally, I had to respond in kind. But Gilda was a generous partner, spinning about into sixty-nine position so that I could enjoy another encounter with her mouth organ while she received her initial oral inoculation. The session was all the sweeter knowing that on this day the real reunion festivities would begin. That was sure to mean multiple ass for all of the class—an appetizing prospect to say the least.

Pantyless as always, Gilda and I wore miniskirts and skin-tight pullovers to the opening ceremonies. They were being held outdoors in the soccer stadium and athletic field on the edge of the campus.

"Careful how you sit, honey, or your beaver may be smiling at the wrong person," I warned Gilda.

"Speak for yourself," she countered. "Your cunt is sticking out like a curly identification badge."

"It's only Mother Nature."

"Mother Nature can be a motherfucker," she retorted. "Better keep your legs crossed, or Dr. Beauregard will be whistling up your Fallopian tubes."

"It might give him another educational degree," I said.

"Like summa come lotta?" she joked.

"We should try to fuck him, just for the fun of it."

"I don't think the headmaster's ever had head in his life," Gilda declared.

"He's married," I pointed out.

"That doesn't even prove he's had his prick in a pussy."

"Madame Beauregard doesn't look like much of a piece," I noted. "Maybe the marriage has never been consummated."

"I saw them both eating consommé at a banquet once," Gilda jested.

"From each other's bowls?" I parried in an effort to top her. "Otherwise it's just unconsummated consommé."

"That's a souper analysis."

"Enough of this bouillabaisse bullshit. They

may well be involved in a platonic relationship."

"There's no tonic in that as far as I'm concerned," Gilda declared. "He might as well be a monk and she a nun."

"Under those circumstances they're both nones. Neither one of them is getting anything."

"They're both intellectuals," she pointed out. "Maybe it's in their fucking brain cells."

"The cranium as crotch?" I questioned pseudo-philosophically.

"Should we flash the gash at him and see how he reacts?" Gilda questioned impishly.

"Front-row seats, huh?" I proposed.

"Let's."

"I'm game."

"No gamier than my beaver."

With this quirky sense of purpose to motivate us, we were among the first to enter the athletic arena to ensure front-row seating directly in front of the podium. The stadium was decorated gaily with banners and balloons along with signs declaring: "Do It for Dumont!" and "Dumonters Do More!"

"I've been doing it for Dumont devotedly since my degree," I told Gilda.

"I don't know who you do it for, but I do it for orgasms—and nothing else."

"You're such a technical bitch," I complained good-naturedly. "Go fuck a balloon."

"They're really heavy-duty condoms," she said with a straight face. "The red ones are for making it in menses."

"Sicky."

"You licky when you sicky," she said in infantile mumbo-jumbo.

We were not alone for long. The stadium began filling up rapidly as the ten A.M. starting hour approached.

"Quick," I said to Gilda. "Go up to the podium before the crowd gets too heavy and check if you can see my cunt from there."

"Good idea."

I assumed my place on the folding chair I'd chosen and spread my legs nonchalantly. Gilda peered over the podium intently, then smiled and made an A-OK signal by forming a circle with her thumb and index finger. She was back in an instant.

"I can practically count the hairs on your pussy."

I grinned. "Old Marcel Beauregard is in for a double dose of raw cunt," I said gleefully. "We'll have him bug-eyed."

"Let's not keep ours spread," Gilda suggested. "Let's just tantalize him with flashes."

"Cross and uncross your legs," I agreed. "Wiggle around in your seat and keep him guessing when the next kaleidoscope of cunt is coming."

We both giggled at the prospect. Dr. Beauregard was a model of propriety, pedantic and largely humorless as far as most of his students knew. It represented true reunion fun to subject him to a bit of pedestal knocking.

Cody Cameron sashayed by, accompanied by her guest, good-looking Eric Blye. She pretended to be speaking confidentially, but intentionally talked loud enough to ensure that we could hear.

"I can't imagine Nicole and Gilda in the front row for *any* school function ever," she declared haughtily. "This must be an orgy—not a reunion."

"Kiss my ashes, Cody," I called out to her.

She smiled and stuck out her tongue.

"Don't do that unless you mean it," I warned

her, "or this *will* turn into an orgy—and you'll be the first on my list."

I'd never made it with her but she was a stunning girl, just snobbish enough to inspire a good fuck.

"If bitches could be witches—which would you be?" she challenged from a distance.

"The bitch which caught your pitch," I retorted, returning her tongue thrust.

"I'll discuss that with you later, Nicky-licky," she teased.

"I think she's hot for your bod," Gilda said as Eric nudged her away.

"Did you ever make it with her?"

"No," she confided. "She loves to play aloof and untouchable."

"Maybe a few years out of school have taught her something."

"You'd like to hit her, wouldn't you?"

I smiled with my lower lip jutting out. "She gets me, right between the legs."

"You take her and I'll take Eric," Gilda proposed.

"I'd rather take both."

"Glutton!"

By now the seats around us were filled. We had little time for further conversation between us as former classmates proffered hands and puckered lips in cheery greetings.

"Damn, you girls look good!" lanky Jeff Whittaker exclaimed. "You look younger'n you did back when I used to visit here in your school days."

"Good living," I responded. "Lots of sex, booze, gambling, and drugs."

"Shit!" he grinned.

"You taking silicone, Gilda?" Simone Breton

inquired casually. "Your tits are sensational, honey."

"Merci," Gilda retorted. "Stop by the dorm later and check them out."

"Am I included?" Jeff jumped in immediately. Dumonters all seemed to have a way of dating amorously opportunistic types.

"Sure," Gilda replied flippantly. "This is nostalgia week, full of fond mammaries."

"I hear there's some real jazzy stuff planned," Simone confided. "On the q.t., of course."

"Like what?" I asked, naturally interested.

"Orgies, sex contests—shit like that."

"I hope so," I declared. "This speechmaking is for the birds."

"Right after this, they're going to have a kind of sex olympics here in the stadium for guests and grads alike. Stay put until old Beauregard exits. Some of the faculty is in on it."

"Dr. Duncan by any chance?" I asked.

Simone looked surprised. "How'd you pick him out of a hat?" she wondered.

"Pay your tuition, and you get intuition."

"I hear he's the one who set it all up," she revealed.

I wondered for a moment why he hadn't mentioned it to me the night before. But then I remembered how totally involved in each other we'd been. Passion had a way of pushing lesser matters out of mind.

"What about Monsieur Tremain?" Gilda inquired.

"Who's he?" Simone responded.

"Ancient history," I told her.

She wrinkled her nose. "Ugh," she said, "maybe that's why I don't remember him. I hate history."

"He might be one of them," Gilda speculated

hopefully. "There are three or four of the younger teachers involved."

"Sounds like fun," I said.

"I do hope René's in the thing," Gilda wished aloud.

"I know *we'll* be in it—for sure," I declared emphatically.

"Me, too," Simone agreed. "If I learned one final thing at Dumont, it's that there's nothing on earth like a good fuck or suck."

"That should be the motto of the school," I laughed.

"*Veni, Fucki, Veni,*" Jeff suggested, showing off his classical education from elsewhere.

"I came, I fucked, I came," Gilda translated. "Not bad."

"I'm getting a hard-on," Jeff declared.

"It's just standing at attention because Dr. Beauregard just walked in."

All eyes went to the speaker's platform, where the headmaster was now taking his place on the dais. He had always been a formal sort of man, rather stiffly attired, but for this occasion he was wearing a maroon sport jacket with a school emblem sewn over the heart. Gray slacks and burgundy loafers completed his surprisingly casual outfit. Dr. Beauregard was a tall, thinnish man with restless eyes and nervous mannerisms. In our years at the Académie, he was known for his strict adherence to the rules and regulations. Was it possible that a change had come over him in so few years?

"He looks different," Gilda said to me.

"Almost human," I agreed.

"We'll put him to the old peeping-pussy test," she snickered. "That'll tell us whether he's got real lead in his pencil or not."

"Don't start until he gets into his speech," I

cautioned her. "Otherwise he might take a duck and put somebody else up there."

"I won't jump the gun. Not unless he pulls it out of his pants."

"Fat chance!" I scoffed. "He doesn't even use public restrooms, I hear. He's that shy with his fly."

"Wouldn't you like to see what he's got?" Gilda inquired with mischief in her eyes. "A pedagogue's prick in public display?"

"Private would be good enough. But let's see what kind of reaction we get this morning."

"Like a rise in the thighs?"

"Shhhh, he's stepping up to the podium."

Polite but limited applause greeted the headmaster's move to center stage. He acknowledged it with a slight, jerky bow and then spread the papers of his speech on the lectern before him.

"Young ladies," he began with a clearing of his throat, "faculty and friends of Académie Dumont, a most joyous welcome to this festive reunion celebrating a decade of honor and achievement, of scholarship and camaraderie in our close-knit and congenial academic community . . ."

Gilda poked me in the side.

"Not yet," I whispered. "He's still in the reading part of his message. Wait until he's sure enough of his memory to look up at the audience."

"What pleasure it brings me to see all of you once again, to read the tales of happiness and success written in your faces," he droned on. "A 'Decade of Dumont' is indeed a cause for celebration; ten years of outstanding leadership in academic studies, the arts and athletics, ten years of contributions to the cause of social consciousness. . . ."

"Double flash," I told Gilda.

Skirts up our thighs, our loins parted, we hit old Beauregard simultaneously with twin servings of pure snatch. His eyes bulged like those of a character in an animated cartoon, and his tongue became hopelessly entangled in his teeth as he sought desperately to regain his elocutionary equilibrium.

"Ar-uh-umm-ahhh," he fumbled about in a word vacuum, a blush rising through him like mercury in a tropical thermometer. "I . . . ahh . . . yes, ah . . . ten years of cunt—that is, I mean . . . *cont*ributions . . ."

There were snickers scattered throughout the crowd by now, heightening the headmaster's visible discomfiture. His neck strained from his collar, giving him the appearance of a cock about to be beheaded.

" . . . As I was saying," he struggled for composure, "these have been extraordinary years at Académie Dumont, years in which no stone has been left unturned in a continuing quest for the finest facilities and curricula attainable . . . "

"Knock him off again," I instructed Gilda gleefully.

She gave him the whole accordion pleating this time and I did likewise, spreading my vaginal ruffles so blatantly that there could be no doubt whatever in his mind about what he was witnessing.

Old Beauregard almost strangled this time, erupting into a choking cough that brought one of his aides rushing to his side with a pitcher of ice water and a glass. The headmaster seized at the aqua as though it were manna from heaven, affording him the luxury of an understandable break to regain his senses. We, of course, were back in prim posture, legs crossed discreetly, avidly attentive to the proceedings.

Dr. Beauregard stepped up once more to resume, this time like a hitter into the batter's box, determined to let nothing distract him from the task at hand. His eyes remained averted throughout the remainder of his address. Only when the applause at conclusion sounded through the stadium did he dare to look our way again.

"Once more?" Gilda questioned.

"No, that would make it obvious. Just be subtle and sit back as if you were unaware you'd done anything to distract anyone from the proceedings, much less Dr. Marcel Beauregard."

We remained the very models of decorum throughout the rest of the welcoming program, despite the steady, penetrating gaze of the headmaster. When it was over, I turned to Simone behind us.

"Did you get the feeling that Dr. Beauregard lost track of himself a few times up there?" I asked her with counterfeit innocence.

"Nicole, you are one bad girl," she smirked.

"Funny," I smiled back at her, "I always thought I was pretty good."

Gilda and I were still laughing hysterically when Dr. Duncan got up to describe the next event on the day's program. I knew one thing for sure—it had been deleted conveniently from Dr. Beauregard's copy. His whole retinue was gone, off to some distracting event of no real significance, while the more carnally creative corps of graduates and their equally erotic guests remained to participate in a cock- and cunt-down to glory.

chapter ten

Our Orgasmic Olympiad got off, so to speak, with a symbolic mass masturbation rite accompanied by the singing of the school song, "Dear Days of Dumont" led by the staff musical director Seymour Flye. Conducting with cock in hand, the elfin bandmaster waved his baton with stirring enthusiasm, climaxing on cue during the final glissando.

Tears were shed by the visiting men and boys— pearly white raindrops of come—while we girls wept inwardly, convulsed with climaxes of nostalgia and joy combined. It was a moving moment, an auspicious beginning for this intimate blending of competition and camaraderie.

Dr. Duncan stood beside me during the opening ceremony, leaving the theatrics to his colleague, Seymour Flye.

"What if Dr. Beauregard learns of this?" I asked.

His smile was wistful. "The sly old fox only

acteth oblivious to what's going on. Actually, nothing taketh place on this campus—well, virtually nothing, thou understandest—without his knowledge."

"You mean he knows this is going on—and permits it?" I asked with no small degree of surprise.

"It's reunion time. There are no undergraduates present. Wouldst thou have come without the prospect of mature merriment?"

"I get you. He just doesn't want to condone it officially, right?"

"Verily. Cast thine eyes toward the planetarium and thou wilt likely see the lenses of the astronomy department's telescopes trained upon the throng."

"With one bulging eyeball belonging to the personal vision equipment of one Dr. Marcel Beauregard," I stated with a certain smug delight.

"Precisely."

Gilda had detached herself from the pair of us to go in search of René Tremain. Roderick had found his name on the clandestine faculty list for the affair, but until now no one had seen him present.

"I'd better take over from Seymour before this turneth into a sing-along," Dr. Duncan decided. "Wouldst thou deign to be my partner in those events which requireth feminine assistance?"

I laughed delightedly. "Such as jacking off for distance?" I inquired impishly.

"And volume as well," he added.

"I'd love it!"

"The laurel wreath shall be ours for certain now," he predicted.

I watched him bound to the stand, admiring his grace and vigor. The combination of those with his soaring intellect had an aphrodisiac effect on my libido. I simply dug bright men with big pricks —that was all there was to it.

"Attention, please, all of thee," Roderick commanded from the stage. "In order to facilitate matters and expedite entries in various events, all of thee must refrain from random intercourse, fellatio, and cunnilingus. They are permissible only in the course of true competitions. To those not participating in specific events, I recommend playing with thyselves or with others immediately at hand. I thank thee, and it's on with the show, on with the blows . . . "

Hands clapped and cheers sounded as René Tremain sprinted abruptly onto the platform wearing only a loincloth and carrying a makeshift torch. He moved breathlessly to the microphone with Gilda, half-stripped and panting, throwing herself at his feet.

"Fellow Dumonters," he began haltingly, "forgive me for launching the events privately without including all of you. My unexpected but welcome partner in these proceedings I'm sure is familiar to many of you—the extravagantly endowed and erotically exotic Gilda Morrow . . . "

"The girl most likely to suck!" someone shouted in remembrance.

"Hooray! Hooray!" others chorused.

"Please?" Tremain pleaded. "We'll never get started at this rate."

"Fuck! Fuck! Fuck!" the crowd chanted jubilantly. "Suck! Suck! Suck!"

Gilda was on her feet now, her gorgeous tits exposed for all to see. It was obvious she had made the most of her ambush of Monsieur Tremain before freeing him to conduct the contests. I waved to her and she flashed a dazzling smile along with the traditional victory signal.

Good for her, I thought. Now she would be *cunt*ent and leave me to my devices with Dr. Duncan.

When the noise subsided, René returned to the mike. "Before everyone is tapped out, we'll hold the He-men Semen Weigh-in at the tables to the right of the field. The object of this competitive event is to extract the maximum amount of sperm possible from the entrants via vigorous masturbation—not by the producer himself but by placing himself in the hands of a female partner. Girls, get your guys and as they say in the vernacular, 'Beat his meat till it spits white heat.' Good luck, welcome, and come well to all of you . . ."

Like a herd of wild mustangs, everyone galloped over to the long row of adjoining folding tables erected on the turf. Minute scales from the chemistry department were spotted at intervals along the expanse, and each entrant was given a standard, lightweight plastic cup in which to catch his come. The girls would be busy with both hands performing the pumping action needed to mine the mellow mucus from the bottom of their partner's balls.

"I held back during the opening anthem," Dr. Duncan confided to me. "Some of the others bleweth away their chances in this event."

"Good thinking, Rod," I told him. "It takes a lot of balls to come out on top in this."

"Is everyone set?" René called out from the head of the elongated table. Gilda had his cock firmly in hand, her left hand clutching his testicles as though they were a sack of jewels.

"Ready, ready, ready," echoed down the line.

"Ladies and gentlemen," Monsieur Tremain declared dramatically, "jerk to the glory of Dumont!"

With several dozen pricks being pounded simultaneously a kind of prurient percussion was produced. Slip, slap, slurp, slush, the cocks seemed to chorus en route to detonation.

"Faster!" Roderick demanded.

"I'm jerking as fast as I can," I retorted. "Besides, this is for volume, not speed."

"I cometh more abundantly through swift friction."

He held his cup near the mouth of his cock, the dolphinlike smile somewhat askance from the flogging of my fist. Several others had come already and were submitting their loads for weighing.

"Let me know when you're going to blow!" I gasped as the swelling seemed to increase, pushing at my firm grip.

"Now!" he grunted, arching backward.

I squeezed his cock like a hose and aimed the nozzle into the cup. It was important not to lose one milligram of the precious prick juice.

"Aughhh!" he groaned as the oysterish globules spilled from the end of his organ and splashed against the bottom of the cup.

"Keep coming!" I urged him, resuming milking his meat.

"That's all of it," he declared as a lone pearl surfaced reluctantly at the tip.

I forced it to break its cling and drop amidst the puddle in the cup.

"It's a good-looking load," I commented, writing his name on the side of the container to prevent mix-ups.

"Merci beaucoup," he replied with obvious satisfaction over his performance.

It was good—but not quite good enough. We finished second to Eric Blye and Cody Cameron.

"It's the age difference," Rod conceded with a measure of disappointment. "The come of youth is the come of copious quantity."

"Maybe we should skip the trajectory competition, then," I suggested. "I heard Simone's guest, Jeff Whittaker, say he could put out a candle at forty paces."

"The truth shall make me flee," Dr. Duncan laughed. "I'll confine myself to judging that event."

Simone Breton came over to congratulate Roderick on his showing in the opening event. "The faculty is now the *fuck*alty, thanks to you."

"Thou art partnering with one Jeff in the distance competition, art thou not?"

"I shall be at the throttle, Professor."

"Good luck. I hear the lad possesseth a powerful instrument."

"I'll say," she agreed. "You should fuck him sometime, Nicole."

I winked at her. "The reunion is young, and so am I."

"Let me know and I'll stage the show," she responded casually.

"How did Gilda and René do?" I asked Rod after Simone was gone.

"My informants tell me poor René performeth pitifully. His vial of viscosity was such a sorry sample 'twas barely ample to register on yon scale."

"Sure, Gilda fucked the hell out of him just before the contest."

"The bare-assed cuntessa," he noted drolly.

"And the barefoot cocksman."

"No, the man hath no more than three-fourths of that amount, pray note."

"Nine inches is a fistful of fornicating flesh, by anybody's standards."

"But not, dear lass, a foot," he reminded me.

"I deal in generalities when it comes to genitals."

As expected, Jeff easily won the jerk-off for distance, achieving a spectacular arcing nine feet three inches. Simone proudly took snapshots of his victorious organ and promised copies to all classmates who wrote her for them. I declined, having more portraits of pricks in my photo collection than I remembered their identities.

Everyone entered and everyone was on his or her own in the Champagne Shower event, which consisted of urinating in clear plastic pails to determine "the biggest pisser in Dumont's piss-tory." I enjoyed the competition even though I failed to place in the bladder derby. Watching all the guys and gals peeing their pricks and pussies out was more fun than a picnic. A hefty anony-mous guest took the title with a frothy flow of more than two liters of his own vintage piss. I fled the area when some of the wilder Dumonters and their dates began throwing their buckets at one another. It took almost half an hour to restore order, leaving several dozen alumnae thoroughly drenched with the chablis of fellow graduates and guests.

"That was shameful," Dr. Duncan com-mented. "It succeedeth in throwing a wet blanket over the festivities hence."

"Forget it, all parties get out of hand at times. Let's enjoy the rest of the day as though it had never happened."

"Something like that could motivate Dr. Beauregard to cancel the entire reunion," Rod said clearly and with no Elizabethan overtones.

I entered the Beauty *Cunt*est and won by a pubic hair over Gilda and Cody Cameron.

"You owe me a suck for that," Cody whispered after a blue ribbon had been placed over my vagina.

"You name the time and place and I'll be there."

"This afternoon," she said. "Right here.

81

There's going to be a Muff-Diving Marathon and I want you between my legs."

I smiled back at her. "Let's face it, that's the best proposition I've had all day."

"I'm entering us as a team," she declared.

"I'm with you."

Lunch was a gourmet picnic with checkered tablecloths spread over the tables where the semen competitions had been held. The food was superb and everyone ate passionately, devouring the pâtés, canapés, veal, and chicken with the ardor of participants in fellatio and cunnilingus.

But the lingering lure of the afternoon was the endurance contest in cunnilingus. Dr. Duncan was disappointed that I had chosen to enter as Cody's companion, then elated when he learned that he could still qualify as my sucking supplicant by enrolling us as a three-member team. In specific and succinct language, that meant that he would eat me while I ate Cody.

The rules were strict: no emergence from the cunt of one's collaborator until one wished to drop out. The choreography of the clitoris was to continue like a dance marathon until the moment of exhausted defeat.

We picked our spot carefully for comfort, Cody positioning herself on a rise that allowed me to wedge my face easily between her thighs and still provide an ample spread of my cunt for Rod. He lay prone in the grass, flexing his tongue to test its range and most effective position.

"Get relaxed," Cody urged. "It's going to be a long sucking night."

"If you have to go at any time," I told her, "just let loose. I'll lick my way right through it."

"The same applieth to thee and me."

"I don't want to wash you out of the race," I laughed. "I'll try to *cunt*rol it."

"It's all caviar and champagne to me," he insisted. "I thrive on it."

Gilda had her René trapped between her legs, her features reflecting her bliss. I waved to her just before the marathon began, but she was clearly in seventh heaven and oblivious to everyone but the man at her beautiful buff base.

"Suck away!" came the signal and dozens of tongues began humming.

Cody had a pussy like a panther, glossy and sleek. Her whole body was lathed for love and nowhere was it more finely crafted than in her vibrant cunt. My tongue set a fast pace at first—much too fast to maintain over a long haul. I realized that after driving her to a cluster of quick climaxes.

"Easy, baby, easy," she cautioned in her silky voice.

I slowed my tonguing tempo after that, following the pace set by Rod in me. It amounted to a lazy lapping that was cumulative in its effect. I came at regular intervals, but not with exhausting wildness as might be my wont under other circumstances.

"Suck it sweetly," she murmured from time to time.

Of the three of us, she was the only one who could talk. Any verbal communication from either Rod or me meant instant disqualification.

Sundown came and went; then dusk settled into twilight with no *cunt*estants dropping out. The field lights were turned on when darkness overwhelmed the atmosphere to make sure there was no cheating. Cody actually slept for a time, a luxury that neither Roderick nor I could afford.

A half-moon joined us a few hours before midnight, silvering the couples and trios locked in oral embraces. It was not until well after midnight that the first dropouts left the field.

"I sucked myself silly," I heard one boy apologize to his partner near us. "I'm too tongue-tired to go on."

Rod's mouth organ was playing a much slower tune, too, by this time. But I was truly surprised when he withdrew his tongue about ten after three A.M. and announced he was finished.

"My tongue is untethered," he declared wearily, "it sucketh no longer."

"Go stick it in a bottle of cognac," Cody advised him. "That'll bring it back to life."

"Nicole doth endure," he noted as he rose and stretched himself.

"She's always been remarkable," Cody said as if I weren't present. "I've always admired her beauty and tenacity."

"Thou hast taste, and she hath taste. Hers is on my tongue forever."

Cody chuckled softly. "We're still in the running. There are only half a dozen couples left."

As she spoke, two more pairs conceded defeat by rising, breaking the oral contact between them.

Peering over her dark pubic hairs, I watched as the sky became littered with the pink and red and violet ribbons of dawn. A little while later, a blood-red sun peeked over the horizon. My tongue barely moved at all by now, resting like a fish in a coral cave, letting its fins keep it afloat.

"Only one other couple, baby," Cody informed me. "Hang in there and we've got it made."

But the muffing marathon had to be called eventually, when it threatened to run into the following day's program. Cody and I, along with Simone Breton and Jeff Whittaker, were declared the co-champions of cunt licking in a four-way division of the title.

How long had we lasted, Jeff and I, in the

canyons of our partners' cunts?

"Eighteen hours, twelve minutes, and thirty-two seconds," the timekeeper reported. "That might be more than a school record—it could be a world record."

"I don't think so," I disagreed. "Once in Lapland, an Eskimo ate me for almost two days."

"Appropriate *cunt*ry for it," Cody joked.

"Let's go bathe our tongues in champagne," I suggested. "There's a long day ahead."

"Amen," Jeff agreed.

Day Two of Reunion One promised to be a different kind of endurance test for the four of us—just trying to stay awake.

chapter eleven

Seminar, seminar.

I liked the ring of it—so close to semen and semantics, two special loves of mine.

"Open roundtable discussions," the program delineated, "in matters of recreational interest to the esoteric elite of Académie Dumont, led by Monsieur Philip Legrand, renowned author of *Giving Head, The Fuck Factor,* and *Going Down.* The initial topic under discussion beginning at ten A.M. will be 'Erotic Impulses and Exotic Responses.' "

"My kind of course," I said to Gilda, who was studying the announcement over my shoulder.

"Have you heard of him? I like the sound of his books."

"He's almost as famous as my friend, Charles Leroux," I replied.

"You still call him your friend after he practically branded you a demimondaine in his last book? I'd kick him in the crotch until he wouldn't be able to use his cock for anything but a bookmark."

"Gilda, Gilda," I sighed, "you have no sense of humor at times. Charles explained it all to me. It's just a piece of sophisticated satire—tongue-in-cheek chic that does nobody any harm."

"His tongue will never go in my cheek, or any other orifice on my body."

"You don't even know him! He might have been in you already."

"Without my knowledge?" she scoffed. "Do you think I've gone deaf, dumb, blind, and numb?"

"He's on the Riviera a lot when we're there, dear girl," I responded airily, "and you know what a penchant you have for wrapping your gams around suave, gorgeous men."

"*He's* suave and gorgeous?" she questioned. "Then whoever took his picture for the jacket of *The Adultery Commitment* should be sued for photographic malpractice."

"My, the fangs are out early this morning. Could it be attributed to the early dropout of Monsieur Tremain from the cunnilingus competition last night?"

"I despise victors who boast of their conquests," she retorted, turning away.

"At any rate, and despite the poor portrait of Charles on the dust jacket of his novel—he is a handsome and charming man."

"I'll accept your word," she replied. "You've tasted enough men to have developed a good and discerning taste."

"Very magnanimous of you, darling," I reacted, giddy from weariness and champagne.

The first meeting of the morning was being held

in Lyon Hall, several buildings down from the residential cottage where we were staying with two other alumnae. Gilda got over fits of pique rather more quickly than I did, so she was in a different and better mood as we took the winding path to the hall.

"Did you catch the speed competitions yesterday?" she asked in a considerably less strident and definitely more buoyant voice.

"Part of them. Rod didn't want to enter, so I was distracted during a portion of the finals."

"Then you didn't see the winner do his thing?"

"No." I admitted.

"Nicole," she gushed, "you wouldn't believe it. Absolutely fantastic!"

"Who was it?"

"Some guy who came with a gal who graduated five or six years ahead of us with a head as bald as his prick."

"We'll give him an Indian name then," I kidded. "Bald Prick."

"Call him whatever you want, but he got his totem pole up and off in only ten seconds, I swear to God."

"You mean from soft to hard and pop in that period of time?" I asked, funneling my face in disbelief.

"I mean his cock was limp as warm taffy when the bell sounded, then got hard as rock candy and shot off. A good load, too."

"Let's steer clear of him," I remarked, still a bit skeptical of the time statistic. "Ten-second fucks aren't worth the bother to clean the mess."

"Oh, he claims he can last, too," she said. "According to him, it's all a matter of will."

"Dumont grads attract strange species of characters," I replied. "Sometimes I think we're closer to normal than any of them."

Her emerald eyes flashed in my direction. "Do you really believe that?"

"No."

"Neither do I."

Philip Legrand proved to be a fluttery, butterfly sort of man, slight, intense and sputtering with kinetic energy. My first impression made me wonder how he managed to sit still long enough to write one book, much less three best-sellers. A small crowd had already gathered about him, peppering him with pre-seminar questions.

He stopped abruptly as Gilda and I entered the room. "One of you has to be Nicole."

Gilda and I stood side by side, taken aback by his comment.

"Which, then?" I asked.

"You," he decided spontaneously.

"Why?"

The author adjusted his glasses and smiled nervously. "With no intent whatever to detract from the undeniable allure of your companion, I was simply told to look for the most beautiful girl I'd ever seen. That made you Nicole."

"No, monsieur," I denied with a poker face, "I am Gilda Morrow, and this young lady next to me is Nicole."

Our fellow alumnae caught on to the playful switch quickly enough not to upset the apple cart —only the guest moderator. He was taken aback visibly by his imagined mistake.

"I am sorry." He wrang his hands. "My apologies to you both. You are both extremely beautiful regardless of identity."

I couldn't let him suffer any longer. His distress was too evident and embarrassing.

"Monsieur Legrand?" I said from the middle of the floor.

"Yes?"

"It is I who should apologize to you for making a travesty of your kind remarks. I am Nicole, just as you deduced."

His face brightened. "No harm done. A bit of levity is always welcome as preliminary to serious discussion."

"Then you forgive me?"

"Certainly. In fact, I bring you fond greetings from a mutual friend of ours, Charles Leroux."

"Charles," I bubbled. "Gilda and I were just talking about him."

Philip Legrand smiled. "Yes, it was he who gave me that very fitting description of you."

"How sweet of him," I cooed.

"Right in the balls," Gilda whispered under her breath. "Remember what I told you."

"Please be seated, Nicole and Gilda," the guest author-moderator urged us. "It's time to get our informal give-and-take under way."

We did as requested, assuming seats next to one another and directly across from Legrand.

"Before we begin in earnest," Philip told his mixed audience of several dozen, "I wish to congratulate the crack athletes who participated in the quasi-Olympiad event of last evening—and the victors who survived the crack of dawn to taste the fruits of victory . . ."

His salute was greeted by laughter and a round of muffled applause.

"In keeping with that spirit," he continued, "I'd like to invite all of you to masturbate freely during our discussion. I've discovered through experience that it helps in keeping a calm perspective relative to erotic dialogues."

The tabs of an undeterminable number of zippers moved south at the invitation, providing ready access to restless genitalia.

"It is a universal experience, thus familiar to all

of us, to see or meet by chance a person to whom one feels an immediate and intense sexual attraction," Philip postulated. "When that sensation overwhelms someone, how best should he or she cope with the emotional floodtide . . . ?"

Hands shot up, and a variety of responses, ranging from raunch to reason, resulted.

"Tickle her palm and ask her for a fast fuck," one guest suggested.

"Put your tongue in her ear and your hand on her crotch," another proposed.

"I would harden my nipples and purposely stumble and drill them into his chest," a bosomy blonde whom I didn't know declared.

"A carnal confession is best," another girl volunteered. "Tell the guy you've got the hots for him, and ninety-nine chances out of a hundred he'll be ripping your main seam before you have time to get your legs apart."

The banter went on, easily and erotically, through a gamut of subjects exploring the nutritious aspects of sex ("There's more protein in the juice of a prick than there is in a pound of prime beef" one scholar contended), novelty capers like being "winged-off" by flies shorn of their wings and left to wander atop cocks and cunts, discussion on how to subdue untimely erections ("It can be embarrassing when taking communion," one young man confessed), miscellaneous trivia like the fact that the beaver is Canada's national animal ("No wonder there's still so much wild territory up there," noted someone), agreement on the moderater's contention that "Sucking is a sweet science," and a wide-ranging dialogue on the virtues of fellatio, cunnilingus, anal intercourse, bisexual activities, and the like.

"I think we've come to the end of our time," Philip announced somewhat reluctantly since he seemed to be enjoying the ebb and flow of conversation as much as anyone, "and I trust you've all had time to come. Thank you most sincerely for being so vociferous and attentive, so educational and open-minded. Good luck and good fuck to you all."

The lusty applause ended suddenly with the surprise appearance of Dr. Marcel Beauregard at the head of the table. There were a few gasps and the quietly urgent sound of zippers being hastily yanked up as he cleared his throat to speak.

"Graduates of Académie Dumont, dear alumnae, and all friends," he said, smiling benignly, "unbeknownst to you I have been sitting nearby, out of sight, listening to this remarkable round-table discussion. I am struck and pleased by the honesty and forthrightness of your perceptions and the maturity of your conclusions. It is a credit to the fine educations you've received here, and I particularly want to congratulate the distinguished novelist Philip Legrand for the manner in which he moderated this fascinating forum. That is all I have to say for now—other than that I trust you will continue to enjoy the entertaining activities planned for you during this grand reunion week . . ."

A stunned audience of former students and their male companions reacted with enthusiastic whistles and applause. The same thought was shared by all of them: Could this possibly be the strict moralist who had presided over our educations with such unrelenting authority and discipline? Gilda and I got our answer immediately.

"Ah, Nicole and Gilda," Dr. Beauregard intercepted us near the doorway, "may I have a word with the two of you in private, please?"

All at once we were like undergrads again, summoned to the summit. There was no doubt in my mind regarding the reason for the headmaster's request. Nor could there be in Gilda's.

"Why yes, of course, Dr. Beauregard," I stammered.

"Gilda?" he directed his piercing eyes to her.

She shrugged halfheartedly. "Sure," she gulped. "Why not?"

"There's a small office at the end of Lyon Hall," he said. "Why don't we go there?"

We both nodded in unison. "Okay."

Dr. Beauregard clicked the latch behind us, locking the door from the inside. Were we going to be paddled, spanked on our rumps, in the time-honored tradition of Dumont discipline?

"I think you both know why I've summoned you here," he declared with a cryptic smirk. "You made the delivery of my opening address to the reunion gathering a most difficult chore—"

"But, Doctor—" I interrupted.

"Please?" he held up his hand. "Let me finish. A most difficult chore, yes—but also a most deliciously delightful one. Therefore, by the rules of tit-for-tat, here is your punishment—a hundred lashes with my own precious whip . . . "

With that the headmaster tore his towering cock from his pants and fell against the single desk in the office. The prick stood like a red steeple waiting to be jacked.

"Both of you, genuflect and express suitable oral remorse for your deeds," he instructed.

"Now I understand why you hold the title of headmaster," I murmured. "Look at the head on that, Gilda."

She was already doing penitence on his prick, her tongue lavishing liquid licks along its veined tower. I knelt beside her and together we slathered it with spit before alternately sucking the plump crimson crown.

"You are gifted young ladies," Dr. Beauregard proclaimed, his hands knighting our heads. "Never have I seen such inspirational incisions as those exhibited by the two of you at the opening ceremonies . . . "

His cock continued to swell until it seemed on the verge of bursting.

" . . . I vowed then and there that I must anoint you with the warmth and wisdom that God has granted to me," he declared, "not only in intangible intelligence but in liquid form as well . . . "

My eyes met Gilda's over the surface of his veined cock. Hers reflected what I knew, too—that Dr. Beauregard was on the very brink of orgasm.

"Here then," he said with hoarse urgency, "is the truth and the glory onto you forever and ever. Amen!"

A fleur-de-lis of come spewed from the tip of his prick, a fireworks display of glistening white, that rained down upon the upturned faces of us both. A messianic rapture spread over his features as he leaned there long after the last pearl had hung suspended from his corona before dropping to the floor.

He insisted that we give him a close-up repeat performance of our stadium flashing routine, then was equally adamant about eating us both. By the time Dr. Beauregard finally released us, chastened but far from chaste, we had gone several unexpected degrees upward in our continuing higher education.

chapter twelve

My regard for Dr. Beauregard had risen like his cock after our *cunt*frontation in Lyon Hall. What a modern, contemporary, liberal, and humane man he truly was. No wonder there was no school on the Continent—nor in the world, for that matter—to equal Académie Dumont! It sent a new surge of reunion joy through me as I *cunt*emplated it, finger on my clit, before arising the next morning.

Gilda, on the bed next to mine, reposed in a lazy spread-eagled posture, a humming vibrator cozily sandwiched between her thighs.

"Wasn't he something?" I asked her, although she gave no indication she was truly awake.

"Bozo?" she asked dreamily, using a secret pet nickname for the headmaster. "I never knew he had it in him."

"Or *on* him," I noted. "He's pretty well hung for a Ph.D."

"Maybe that stands for Doctor of Phallicism," she conjectured in jest.

"Could be. Whatever it connotes, the old boy came through with flying colors."

"He came, but there was only one color flying, and that was pearly white."

"I was surprised how virile he was," I reflected. "He would have finished high in the ejaculation weigh-in."

Gilda smiled, her eyes closed. "I don't think he's quite up to wide-open performing. After all, he does have to be selective to maintain the dignity of his office."

"No man has dignity with a hard-on," I philosophized.

"Just as no man looks dapper sitting on the crapper."

"Why must you get scatological?"

"Now that you excremention it, who gives a shit?"

"Gilda, Gilda," I said plaintively, "why can't you hold your tongue like a lady?"

"I can't suck that way," she replied. "So who wants to be a lady?"

"Put the vibrator in your mouth for a change and maybe some good will come of it."

"I have a good come ready to roll in my vertical mouth just about now."

"Let's hear you moan about it."

She squeezed her eyes tightly shut and rammed the replica of a cock deep into her hairy hole. "Ooooohhhhh!" she groaned and then began corrugating convulsively.

"Pop goes the weasel," I said, "or make that the beaver."

"God, that was a good, healthy come," she reported after several moments of blissful silence.

"Let me have it while it's still hot with your juice."

She slid the long five-celled dildo out of her luscious laceration and handed it to me. I licked it briefly, savoring the flavor of her sensual syrup, and then plunged it into my own aroused pussy, swallowing almost half of it in one gulp of my cunt.

"Did you get any of Philip Legrand?" Gilda asked as my labia clutched at the pulsating pseudo-prick.

"What makes you ask that?"

"I think your friend what's-his-name, the author, probably gave you a big body buildup, and Legrand was all hot to get laid."

"You mean Charles? He wouldn't do that. He's discreet."

"After that *roman à clef* he did on your cleft?" she scoffed. "Come, now, honey, you're not that naïve."

"No, but I'm going to come now just the same," I reported in shallow breaths.

Gilda leaned over and sucked one of my nipples as I spun into a dizzying sequence of orgasms.

"For fuck's sweet sake," I gasped, "that was mellow, ooooeee, mellow."

"Pancho Gomez had that specially designed and made for me down in Rio. It just takes five regular flashlight batteries."

"What a potent prick! Next time you're down there, get one for me will you?"

"A Pancho or a dildo?"

"Panchos I can get like tacos."

"I'll get you the one you want," she promised.

"Thanks. About Philip—how could I have done anything when we were both with Bozo?"

"That's right," she recalled. "I was just curious, that's all."

"You know what curiosity did to the pussy, don't you?"

"Mine is immortal."

"Drop the 't' from that and I'll accept the claim."

"Snide bitch!" she hissed.

"Cunt!"

We both enjoyed making curt, disparaging remarks about each other. All in fun, of course.

The day's schedule was crowded as usual with varied events and activities. There were picnics and cocktail parties, games and dances, concerts and meetings all over the campus. It was literally impossible to attend them all. But both of us were intrigued by one offering—a tent meeting "to afford fellow graduates of Académie Dumont with the once-in-a-lifetime opportunity to become franchisees in a unique new erotic venture headed by a devout friend of Dumont, Thomas Riddle."

"Tommy Riddle!" I exclaimed when I read his name. "He's the boy who used to sit in on the Visitors Days functions with his cock out between his legs, remember?"

"How could I forget?" Gilda replied. "Everybody in our senior class called him 'Cannon.' "

"He had a prick like a horse," I recalled. "He used to stroke it as if it were an animal."

"Never got caught either," Gilda remembered, "or he would have been banished from the guest list forever."

"Wonder what kind of business he's in?" she mused.

"Didn't we secretly vote him The Boy Most Likely to Have His Seeds Sucked?" I asked, recalling the accelerated mischief of our last semester.

"Right. That was the same week we were voted the Girls Most Likely to Suck."

"*You* were voted."

"And you," she insisted.

"Your memory bank is tilted, but who cares?

Let's check into Tommy's swindle just for the fun of it.''

"He always was a con man. A different girl had him as her guest every week."

"And a cunt man, I hear," I added. "But I suppose that's inevitable for a guy as hung as he is."

"I don't think I could handle him," Gilda said thoughtfully.

"Bullshit! Your cunt is all wool and a yard wide."

"You bullshitting bitch!" Gilda punched my shoulder. "I'm tight in the twat and you know it."

"The only way your cunt could be tight is if you got it drunk!"

We began throwing pillows at one another, then turned to wrestling on the floor. Eventually, with much huffing and puffing, I managed to pin her arms down. Sitting astride her, I negotiated the terms of surrender. "Now listen, baby doll, no more arguing over widths and depths, no more sly punches, no more scatological shit. Understand?"

"Go fuck yourself!"

"I already did that." I smiled in spite of myself. "We have to get going if we're going to make the sales pitch by Riddle-diddle. Promise you'll behave if I let you go."

"I'll bite your butt."

"You'll bite the dust if you do."

"Let me go!" Gilda shouted.

"Shhhh! You'll have the security cops up here."

Reluctantly, Gilda agreed to comply with my stipulations. "You're worse than a butch dike. Bossy bitch!"

"Watch it," I cautioned.

It was all good-natured rowdyism, but sometimes in the past the tomfoolery had gone too far and resulted in temporary hard feelings. But on this sunny morning, we were both in exceedingly high spirits, delighted with everything about the reunion so far. And we were getting along better than we had in ages.

On our way to the candy-striped tent on campus, Gilda asked about Aunt Valerie. "Have you called that sweet, nutty aunt of yours since we got here?"

"No, I really should have invited her. We could easily have arranged some cock-dueling exhibitions among the guests and faculty for her foundation."

"To say nothing of sixty-nines for her society."

"The week's already half over," I lamented.

"It was just a thought." Gilda dismissed the notion.

"I should call Erich and Ulrica, too," I remembered. "It's just that we've been so busy all the time."

"It's difficult to carry on a decent, intelligible conversation with a cock or a cunt in your mouth."

"Don't whet my appetite."

"Don't wet my pants," Gilda volleyed.

"You don't wear panties."

"Then don't wet my pubes," Gilda corrected herself.

"They're always damp."

"Simmering."

Bantering, we entered the festively decorated tent. Multicolored balloons hung suspended from the top of the canvas shelter. On closer examination, they proved to be not the traditional type of circus balloons but gaily painted condoms.

"I hate those things," I declared.

"It's like getting fucked with your clothes on."

"I won't let a man fuck me that way," I said with conviction. "Either he skins it off—or it's no skin off my twat."

"You should suggest that as a cause for Aunt Valerie."

"That would be a worthwhile one for a change. Wear rubbers on your feet—not on your foot."

"Hey, good slogan, except that most guys don't have twelve inches."

"Tommy has," I reminded her. "So, for the moment, it's apropos."

"You're impossible!"

The rows of folding chairs inside were rather sparsely populated, as might be expected. Nobody came to a reunion to hear a promotional pitch for investing money in an untested franchise scheme. But nevertheless there were a dozen or so people on hand, either out of curiosity or because they might have known Tommy casually as we had. His phallic reputation was as widespread as his cock was long.

I looked about and waved to Jeff Whittaker, who was with Simone Breton again. That was beginning to look like a real romance. I thought the same about Eric Blye and Cody Cameron, who were busy deep-throating one another several rows behind us. Seymour Flye was there, too, sans musicians or instruments. All the hoopla apparently would be coming direct from Tommy's loquacious mouth.

"Maybe Peter will be interested in investing in this," Gilda speculated.

"Without even knowing what it is, I'd tend to say no. He really isn't the franchise type—not unless he owns the patent."

A pair of leggy, scantily clad girls moved about the tent serving champagne from trays. At least Tommy had learned something about softening an audience since we'd last seen him at our graduation, having relied previously mostly on the power of his prick. He suffered from a tendency toward excess in speech as well as sex, but he could be ingratiating when he was in the proper mood, as I recalled.

"Here he comes," he announced himself as he swept into the tent in long, loping strides, "the one and only Tommy Riddle, a conundrum surrounded by condoms. How are all you beautiful people this lovely morning?"

He literally skipped onto the small platform serving as his stage. Next to him was a table with several large locked cases obviously containing samples of his products.

"Let me test my memory for beauty for a moment before I begin," he said, spinning about as he spoke. "Unless I'm mistaken, that's Nicole right there sitting next to Gilda and that's Cody next to—I don't retain men's names nearly as well, so please forgive me if I muff it and pardon the expression as well—Captain Blye, who trades under the name of Eric. Right? Hey, I must be turning bi recalling that one. And that's sweet Simone over there with that tall drink o'water named Jeff. . . . "

He went on through the audience displaying a remarkable ability to remember names and faces of people he'd met only casually and occasionally, missing only one.

"You're wondering, I'm sure, just what sort of sucker trap I've got set for you, aren't you?" he continued. "Well, if turning you all into millionaires constitutes suckering, then suck away, I say, don't you?"

There was scattered applause and a few shouts of "yea!" confirming his contention.

"Let me make this short and sweet since I have a rep around this feminine campus for going the long way," he declared with a grin.

There were giggles and snickers now, visibly pleasing him.

"I want you Dumonters to get in on something with me that's so sensational in its potential that you'll have an orgasm when I tell you about it." He waved his arms for emphasis. "It has to do with sex, which has to do with just about everybody and everything. Don't you agree?"

"Amen!" someone shouted.

"Hallelujah!" called out another.

Tommy resumed his spiel. "Sounds like a revival meeting, and in a way that's what it is, a revival of real passion in romance, a rebirth of the birthmaking process—with or without the by-product . . ."

"Oh, baby!" Gilda cried aloud.

"No baby," Jeff responded. "Just the fun part!"

Tommy's eyes gleamed at the audience partic-ipation. It meant they were with him, responding to his words.

"There's so much natural beauty here, so much God-given handsomeness among you people, you'd think nothing more could be done to enhance the sex appeal of those present. But I say that's a false assumption. I say I can take any one of you and make you so much more desirable that you're liable to fall in love with yourselves all over again . . ."

"Right on!" Simone hooted.

"Are you ready?" Tommy questioned dramat-ically.

"Ready!" the whole audience chorused.

Tommy unlocked the large cases with a flour-ish, propping them up to reveal rows and rows of tubes, jars and gadgets in orderly succession.

"The Vee Line!" he declared proudly. "The Vee Line of cunt cosmetics and cock cosmetology. Makeup for your muffs and lotions for your lobs. Exciting, isn't it?"

Everyone seemed stunned. No one knew what to expect, and yet no one had expected what they got. It took several moments for me and apparently everyone else just to ascertain a reaction. I didn't know whether to laugh or be serious. Surely he had to be serious—it was too elaborately set up to be a practical joke.

"Think about it, ladies and gentlemen," Tommy filled the silence with no loss of enthusiasm, "a complete line of the finest creams, lotions, and color makeup to compliment the loveliest of pussies and pricks. Even the name—Vee—was chosen with the crotch in mind: the vulval triangle, the masculine groin . . ."

"It's a good thing Aunt Val isn't here, after all," I whispered to Gilda. "She'd probably blow the family jewels on some God-forsaken locations."

"This would be a natural for her," Gilda said, her smile giving me no clue whether she was serious or not.

I rolled my eyes to express how farfetched it all seemed to me. But apparently about half of those present really were genuinely interested. They were the first to respond when Tommy asked for volunteers for a demonstration. Cody, who might have been more interested in showing off her gorgeous black cunt than in the products themselves, got up first, spreading her blossom wide at Tommy's instruction.

"Maintaining ethical behavior might well be the most difficult part of dealing in these products," he stated as he squeezed one of the tubes. "In fact, you can see for yourselves how hard it is for me right at the moment."

There was no denying that. His cock stood out inside his pants like a flagpole.

"The ointment I'm applying to the lips of

Cody's lovely cunt is called Luscious Labia. It works wonders on those tender and intriguing tissues of the twat," Tommy chattered as he carefully brushed the substance on.

There were other volunteers for demonstrations of such vaginal items as Fruity Fuck, Clit Spit, Cunt Cocoa, Pretty Pubes, Labia Lipstick, and Pussy Pancake. In all, the line included over a hundred different items, most of which he left to a brochure to describe.

"I just want you to get acquainted with the concept," he explained. "This conception of the cunt has nothing to do with childbirth, of course."

Everyone was more or less into the spirit of the occasion by now, freely fondling themselves and their neighbors as genitals *au naturel* became the order of the day. Tommy himself demonstrated the penis potions on his own upstanding model.

"You can decorate yourself like a totem pole with the shades of makeup, and soften the hardest prick with our special moisturizers," he suggested.

"Is there come in any of the products?" Simone questioned in the midst of his phallic presentation.

"Only in the feminine line. There is a modicum of pussy juice in each cream and ointment in the male products."

I tested a touch of muff makeup called Ruby Rape on the outer lips of my cunt, turning it into a vivid purplish crimson. "Anybody want a kiss?" I called out gleefully. There were four immediate volunteers.

Gilda tried a nipple salve that turned her prominent tit tips lushly scarlet and thimble-sized. "Ooooh!" she sighed, "it's like a narcotic."

Tommy confided to her that it contained a smidgin of cocaine. "Allow me to suck them supple again," he volunteered.

In no time at all, the tent was teeming with

suckers and fuckers smearing themselves with carnal cosmetics. Tommy offered no objections—it was all part of the pitch, he explained—and threw his king-sized ruler wholeheartedly into the fray.

What a mess we all were by the time the demonstration was over!

"We look like Indians on a rampage," I declared.

"Look at Tommy's tool," Gilda said. "There never was a totem pole to equal that one for colors."

Together we managed to lick most of it off, succeeding in the process to get lacquered by the exclusive love lotion manufactured in his own spermaries. It was a come-and-go situation. Covered with come, we left, still undecided whether we had been put on to put out—or whether the Vee Line was like his cock, namely, on the up-and-up.

chapter thirteen

It was the guidance counselor, Dr. Lucas Montaigne, who opened the special postgraduate awards ceremonies on the day following the cosmetics debacle in the striped tent. It was as if the whole campus had been painted red in the makeup mayhem. But Dr. Luke, as he was known affectionately to most of us, was as benign as a calico pussycat from the podium of the main auditorium, beaming over the gathering of graduates like a lighthouse beacon, as always oblivious to all bad vibes.

"Children, children," he began in his rich baritone, "what fun we're all having with so many of our dear Dumont family and their friends gathered here once again to celebrate ten wonderful years of enlightened education. Let us bow our heads and make an oral commitment to carry on in this great tradition throughout our lifetimes, come hell or Hiram Walker."

Several of us giggled at his reference to a brand of whiskey, a recognition that brought a delighted smile to his cherubic face. He had a marvelous gift of making light of serious matters, punctuating prayers and sermons as well as ordinary conversation with puns and *bon mots*. Nothing about Dr. Luke, or me either, for that matter, was intentionally sacrilegious. We simply shared a sort of obtuse sense of humor. I adored him because he did possess that extra human quality that made his counseling mission so much more palatable for free spirits like myself.

Immediately after the invocation, the proceedings were turned over to Bozo—I mean Dr. Beauregard. Dr. Luke plopped his plump figure down on a folding chair next to Dr. Duncan and Monsieur Tremain, who were part of the faculty committee making the awards.

"I think René has a hard-on," Gilda whispered.

"That's wishful thinking on your part."

"Look at his crotch."

"A mirage," I declared.

"The only way you could make that mirage disappear is between your legs."

"Are you suggesting that I seduce Monsieur Tremain?" I teased her.

"Hands off! Legs off, too."

"I feel like Venus de Milo. You've chopped off all my limbs."

"When it comes to René, keep your limbs in limbo."

"Listen to what Bozo's blathering about, and stop worrying about the lump in Tremain's lap."

She stuck out her tongue at me and thumbed her nose before turning her attention to the podium. I loved to irk her at times, much as I had done throughout our days at Dumont.

" . . . and therefore, in the light of her achievements in the international galaxy of stars," Dr. Beauregard was preaching, "bringing glamour and renown to Académie Dumont as well as herself, I take extreme pleasure in awarding an honorary Doctor of Divine Dimensions degree to our own delectable alumna, the illustrious Nicole, honoring her request that she be known only by that single sensuous surname . . ."

Cheers and applause rang in my ears. I was genuinely stunned.

"Me?" I questioned in disbelief, pointing at myself as I rose hesitantly.

"You in 3-D," Gilda confirmed. If she was even the slightest bit envious, she conveyed none of it, smiling sweetly at me.

Nicole, D.D.D. Dr. Nicole. The titles ricocheted through my mind as I swiveled through the crowd to the platform. Dr. Duncan had arisen and stood next to Dr. Beauregard, a black gown with purple vestments suspended from his arms.

"Congratulations," he whispered as I approached. "Slip into this to receive your degree."

My dimensions, divine or not, disappeared under the dark robe. Dr. Beauregard placed a mortarboard on my head and then stuck a role of parchment, tied with a purple ribbon, in my hand without releasing his hold on it.

"Nicole," he said solemnly, "by the authority vested in me by the board of trustees of the Académie Dumont and on behalf of the faculty and student body thereof, I hereby present you with the title of Doctor of Divine Dimensions, said doctorate entitling you to be addressed as Doctor and bestowing upon you the academic accreditation implicit in its area of specialization. Congratulations and the very best wishes of all of us . . ."

His kiss was as unexpected as the degree but

from the reaction of the audience it was a popular gesture.

"I—I—don't quite know what to say other than thank you ever so much for this great honor—this great, unanticipated honor I might add. I'll do all I can to live up to it and bring fame and glory to the treasured name of Académie Dumont," I rambled almost without thinking.

"Strip!" someone in the audience shouted. "Show us the divine dimensions!"

"Is there a doctor in the house?" another anonymous voice questioned loudly. "I'm suffering from hardening of the main artery between my legs!"

Bozo chose to ignore the jibes as he'd done all week so far, apparently resigned to a certain amount of reunion ribaldry. After all, we were not students any longer and therefore not really within his realm of authority. As I had noted earlier, he was considerably more relaxed and affable than he'd ever been when we were undergraduates.

There were other degrees awarded, but none to any of my immediate friends. A surprise announcement was the Peter Theophilus Prize in Erotic Architecture, which went to an older grad named Greta Miklaus for a phallic tower scheduled to be erected on campus during the coming year.

"In Greek, the native tongue of our donor, Theophilus means 'dear to the gods,' " Dr. Beauregard explained, "but to us it means 'dear to Académie Dumont.' "

Peter had set up the $10,000 annual award in honor of me, it was disclosed later. That revelation earned me another standing ovation, accompanied by the repeated chanting of my name.

"Nicole! Nicole! Nicole!" my classmates cheered.

"Doctor! Doctor! Doctor!" another segment of the audience shouted.

I didn't know whether to be flattered or embarrassed by this outpouring of accolades and affection. Most of it was sincere, but I suspected some of it was sarcastically and spitefully motivated. Gilda had not convinced me, among others, that she was truly delighted by all the attention I was getting.

"Instead of a school reunion, it's beginning to sound like a Nicole family reunion."

"The absence of Aunt Valerie rules that out," I replied as sweetly as I could.

"She should be here to see her niece put on a pedestal."

"I hardly think that's happened," I retorted.

My blood was simmering at this stage, distracting me from much of the concluding ceremonies. But I did hear the poet laureate award being presented to Simone Breton. In accepting the honor, Simone read one of her brief poems from her winning collection, "Musings and Abusings":

Girls are made of sugar and spice
   and everything nice,
Especially the slice.

It was cute and garnered her a well-deserved round of applause, led by Jeff Whittaker, of course. But Gilda sat on her hands and stared off in the distance during this and all the other closing presentations. Her pique was increasingly apparent, continuing until René Tremain made a last minute dart to the side of Dr. Beauregard, whispering in his ear as he was about to call for the benediction.

"Oh, yes, yes," he was overheard saying to Monsieur Tremain, "I'd almost forgotten. Thank you for reminding me."

René's appearance lifted Gilda momentarily from her funk. She seemed apprehensive as Bozo cleared his throat once more for yet another announcement.

"Dear friends of Dumont, dear members of its family," he began in his standard fashion, "we have one last award to make, one determined by the vote of the faculty alone, in recognition of outstanding qualities of scholastic tenacity, devotion to Dumont, and beauty of physique and philosophy. The first annual Golden Beaver Award is hereby bestowed upon our own sensual, scintillating scholar, the lovely Gilda Morrow . . . "

Gilda recoiled in surprise. I jumped up and hugged her, pulling her to her feet.

"Congratulations, you bitchy beaver," I whispered in her ear.

There were tears in her eyes and a continuing look of disbelief on her face. Seymour Flye sent the band into a stirring march as Gilda, undulating her hips in her naturally erotic way, marched to the stand to accept her trophy.

"Gilda! Gilda! Gilda!" the chorus resumed with two new syllables to enunciate.

"Beaver! Beaver! Beaver!" came the now-inevitable responding chants.

I felt genuinely happy for her—and relieved as well that she had not gone unrecognized and unrewarded. The day now loomed as the happiest of all so far and I could hardly wait to celebrate it with a barrage of galactic orgasms.

chapter fourteen

An original farce, *The Naked Truth*, was to be presented on the evening of the awards ceremonies. It was written by Dr. Duncan and geography professor Claude Reims, and an elated Gilda and I looked forward to it gleefully.

"Professor Reims is a doll," Gilda remarked. "Remember the fun in his classes?"

"Yes, my little Golden Beaver," I kidded her. "He really made geography interesting."

We were at an outdoor pre-theater cocktail party being hosted by the wives of faculty members. They scurried about in long gowns, waiting on us, for a change. That had often been our responsibility toward them when we were students, and I liked this arrangement much better.

"Professor Reims used to have such graphic descriptions of places," Gilda continued to reminisce. "Like calling it 'the hanging cock of Florida' or 'Italy, the boot up Sicily's ass.' "

I nodded, smiling in recollection.

"The Alps were 'the tits of Europe' and the Baltic Sea 'the frigid cunt of the Continent,' " I remembered.

"Imagine what he and Dr. Duncan have concocted for a faculty farce?" Gilda conjectured.

"It should be funny."

"And filthy."

"Risqué," I corrected, "not filthy."

"Pardon my French."

"Which one is Claude's wife?" I wondered, skimming my eyes over the gowned ladies serving drinks and canapes.

"I don't know. I know which one is René's."

"The tall redhead, isn't it?" I asked.

"She must have a pussy like a forest fire."

"They've been married quite a while, so he must like playing with fire."

"That's how you get your glands burned," Gilda quipped.

"I think Roderick's wife is nice," I said between sips of pepper vodka.

"She's very petite. Tall girl, small cunt; small girl, all cunt as the saying goes."

"Rod's got a pretty healthy rod, so she can't be petite all over."

"Probably has one running from her asshole to her belly button," Gilda said.

"How gross!" I reacted. "Wouldn't it be nicer to say from her anus to her navel?"

"Asshole and belly button get right down to basics. Why mince words?"

"Why mincemeat?" I bandied back.

"That wins today's non sequitur award by a country mile."

"A mile of cunt?" I teased her. "It couldn't be that big, Golden Beaver."

"Nothing you say or do can get me down today."

"Not even if I spread it for you with my own little hands?"

"Damn it, Nicole, you know what I'm talking about," she snapped.

"Sometimes you get all tangled up in your tongue and syntax," I commented.

"There's no tax on sin, and the only time I'm tongue-tied is when I'm tied up in a twat."

"But nothing can get you down today," I reminded her.

"If you keep it up, I'll eat you right here in front of all the faculty wives."

"I don't have a cock, so I can't keep it up, now, can I?" I taunted her.

"You're a D.D.D., all right," Gilda replied sharply. "A Damned Dirty Dyke!"

I laughed so suddenly and explosively that I sent half my drink flying onto Gilda. "Oops!" I uttered apologetically.

"Bitch!"

"I'm sorry, baby," I elaborated on my apology. "You always make me laugh when you call me that."

"Now I'll go around smelling like a dipso all night," she complained.

"It's vodka," I assured her. "It'll dry up without a trace."

It did disappear rather quickly, but not soon enough to stem her rising anger.

"You goad me into these situations, and I always wind up the victim. I wouldn't doubt that you arranged to have me get my award last just to gloat over me throughout the ceremonies. Nicole's the best nookie, Nicole's the best lookie, Nicole's got the best cookie—Nicole's this and Nicole's that! Fuck you! Go sit by yourself at the fucking faculty farce and enjoy your own greatness, sitting on your own great ass, feeling your own great gash!''

Gilda's pent-up passions sent me reeling. I couldn't believe the heat of her hostility, as sudden and total as a neutron bomb exploding. She ran off through the startled crowd, none of whom could escape hearing at least part of her verbal assault on me. I was stunned beyond words. There was really no excuse for her behavior, and that realization made me angry enough to drown any disappointment over her abrupt departure. The jealous bitch, I fumed to myself. Go take off and go fuck yourself with your goddamned trophy! Nothing was going to get her down this night, ha! Well, nothing was going to spoil my fun—that was for sure. Let her go sulk in the cottage and then wake up tomorrow crying over having missed the show and begging for forgiveness. I turned to the people nearest to me, smiling broadly. Lifting my glass high, I proposed a toast.

"To the greatest reunion ever held," I proclaimed. "To the greatest faculty and the greatest classmates of the greatest school in the world. I give you the Académie Dumont!''

It eased the tension immediately. Everyone joined me in the salute and in moments the cheery hum of voices chattering was accompanied by the lilt of laughter. Gilda's grandstand act had gone for naught. Everyone present was as determined as I was to have fun—and everything else be damned.

Gilda was forgotten by all, including me, during the gales of laughter that swept the audience in the Edith Piaf Theater, which shared the stone building housing the chapel. Dr. Denton, wearing an enlarged replica of a condom over his head and shoulders, served as narrator throughout, portraying a character aptly named Prick. Prick, in turn, introduced other characters bearing such imaginative names as "Dick Watcher, Graduate Men's Room Attendant and Lord of the Flies" and "Irma Goodfuck, Lay Therapist and Specialist in Pissed-off People."

"Cunt! Cunt! Cunt!" Dick Watcher screams at Irma at one point in the proceedings.

Irma, who was really Latin instructress Lila Beaufort in scanty disguise, responds with: "I'll make you eat those words! How does that grab you?"

"Right in the crotch!"

The sketches came fast and furiously, like ejaculations, with recognizable members of the faculty in such absurd and revealing costumes the gathered graduates grew increasingly hysterical as the evening progressed. Evangeline Hunter, who taught social behavior, sashayed across stage almost naked and answering to the name of Dolores Clitoris.

"Familiarity breeds *cunt*empt," she sniffed grandly. "That's why I despise my cunt!"

The entire cast sang the famous ancient Roman marriage song of Catullus in its entirety, taking particular relish in repeating the key chorus line.

"Holy hymen! Holy hymen!" they sang lustily.

The lines were merry and bawdy, ricocheting off the beams of the theater auditorium. I could scarcely keep up with them as they caromed about my head.

"I want to suck her so bad my teeth ache," a character named Harry Azzole—played by the bandmaster—comments.

"To bare is human, to give head divine," another philosophizes.

"The cat's got her tongue—she's eating pussy," a naked prof observes.

"Yes," responds our feminine hygiene teacher, "look at that little miss muff it!"

I ached with laughter by the time the curtain rang down with the entire cast tearing off the clothes of Dr. Beauregard. Conveniently, the fringe of the velvet drop arrived just in time to save the headmaster from displaying the head of his cock. That involved no disappointment for me since I'd already become intimately acquainted with it a few days earlier.

There was a post-play party in the gym which I left early to check on Gilda. The cottage was dark when I got there. After turning on the lights, I slipped up to our bedroom. There on her bed lay the Golden Beaver statue she had been awarded earlier that day. A note was attached.

Shove it up your ass. I'm gone forever, Doctor.

There was no signature, but there was no doubt who had written it, both in content and calligraphy. Damn her, I thought. She was not going to spoil things for me this time. I simply turned on my spiked heels and headed straight back to the party. Not long after, I was oblivious to everything but the steady succession of cocks knocking at the gateway to my own version of heaven.

I had to put it down as a heady day, in every way imaginable.

chapter fifteen

With Gilda gone, I summoned Aunt Valerie to join me for the final days of the reunion festivities. The way they had been going, they were perfectly suited to her dizzy and daring disposition. She hesitated at first, citing all her crusades and foundation activities, but eventually I persuaded her the action was too amorous to miss.

She arrived in a sheer black jumpsuit, leaving little to the erotic imagination except for a trio of strategically placed leaf designs over her breasts and crotch. From the rear, her deluxe derrière was something to behold. We embraced fervently.

"How marvelous to be with you back at the Académie," she gushed, surveying my physique as she held my shoulders at arm's length. "I do think you're still growing, child. Your chest looks prouder than ever."

"Somehow it swells with pride at the sight of you, Auntie," I told her with tongue in cheek.

Her eyes glinted. "The campus looks absolutely bacchanalian. I never saw so much random sex going on in one place in my life."

"Pure nostalgia," I replied airily. "Old friends getting together once again."

"Nostalgia, perhaps, but pure, no."

"Don't tell me my Aunt Val has become puritanical!" I said with exaggerated disbelief.

"That's why I got into this nun's habit," she kidded, wiggling her shapely buttocks.

"You'll never get in the habit of getting none," I rejoined.

"Nor will you ever cease punning."

"I love to play with words almost as much as with myself."

"Speaking of autoerotism," she segued deftly, "how is my car behaving?"

"I haven't had it out in several days, but the trip here was terrific. What a dream chariot."

"It is a marvelous machine," she agreed. "If I weren't so fond of it myself, I'd let you have it for good."

"You say that about all your loves."

"But I always share," she reminded me. "I've taught you that from earliest childhood, and I hope I've set a good example."

"You have," I assured her. "As one of your campaigns of the past emphasized—blood is thicker than water and much more precious and rare."

"How eloquent!"

"How is the *Sixty-Nine Society* doing?" I inquired.

"Succulently," she reported, a faraway look in her eyes.

"And the *Foundation for Phallic Fencing*?"

"I don't want to sound cocky, but we're already on the verge of staging international dick duels. Isn't that exciting?"

"I get prickly heat at the thought of it."

120

"You're not having fun at your aunt's expense again, are you?"

"I always get a charge out of you, Auntie. You're such a dear!"

"That isn't a play on aunt and antlers, I hope."

I grinned at her. "Very good, Val. I hadn't even thought of that."

"My slogan writers keep me sharp."

"How about a stroll around the alma mater?" I suggested to change the subject.

"I'd like that. I haven't seen some of your classmates since you graduated."

"They're all as devilish as ever, with maybe a little more experience thrown in."

"Nothing that outstrips yours, I'm sure," she commented.

"When it comes to stripping, I strip to come with the best of them."

"Wear something scanty so I don't feel like a naked nymph in this outfit."

"You look tremendous," I told her. "I might have you walk a few feet behind me so I get a little attention, too."

"You flatter like a man, Nicole."

"God knows I've listened to enough of them."

"They can't help it if they have good taste."

"As long as they taste good, too."

Auntie sighed resignedly. "Perpetual antics with semantics."

I accommodated her by donning a pair of short shorts so skimpy they could have passed for lingerie briefs. A halter that halted little more than my nipples completed the outfit, along with spike-heeled pumps to lathe my calves as sensually as possible.

"Ready or not—I'm ready," I announced.

"Ready or not, I'm hot," she almost whistled. "Nicole, you look positively edible."

"Well," I responded flippantly, "right now let's go shopping for leers."

"It's a good thing you already have your diploma," Aunt Val said, "or otherwise they might not give it to you."

"I'll tell you something confidentially. Dr. Beauregard gave it to me the other night."

Her eyes twinkled at the revelation. "In a sheepskin?"

"Bare-cocked. None of those lamb's rubber balloons messing up the friction."

"I never would have thought it of him," she confessed. "I didn't think he was the type."

"He's got eyes and a set of cock and balls. That's all it takes when *cunt*fronted by a naked pussy."

"True," she reflected. "But I thought maybe all that education might interfere with his fuck functioning."

"I want to fix you up with him before this is over. Then you can judge for yourself."

"I'm game," she replied. "I can accommodate sizes up to Ph. D."

"I'm now a triple-D."

"What does that mean?"

"I was awarded a Doctor of Divine Dimensions degree yesterday."

"Are you serious?"

"As serious as when I suck," I responded emphatically. "It's a bona fide honorary degree."

"A doctor in the family!" Aunt Val cried. "I'm so proud of you, Nicole. No wonder your chest was out."

"I think it bent Gilda out of shape. She does give in to the Green Monster now and then."

"You've been friends too long to be jealous of one another."

"The hell with her. Come on, let's go."

The subject of Gilda was scuttled as we sailed

out together to invade the carnival atmosphere on campus, aunt and niece, both ready for a piece.

"Nicole!" a familiar voice called out from under a linden tree.

I peered into the fading sun, trying to distinguish who it was.

"It's me, Cody!"

I pulled at Aunt Val's arm. "You'll like her."

"If you do, I know I will."

Cody was with Eric Blye, as usual, but the group also included Tommy Riddle and Professor Reims.

"This is my Aunt Valerie," I announced. "Watch her. She's armed and dangerous."

"She's legged, assed and titted, too," Tommy observed with typical boldness. "That makes her quadruply dangerous."

"Ignore him, Auntie. Any man who peddles potions for the pubes has to be on the verge of insanity."

"Or at least of inanity," Eric suggested.

"I'm not sure I get it," Valerie confessed.

"You will if you stay in that costume," Tommy commented, unfazed by the putdowns.

"I'll tell you about his muff mascara, et cetera later," I promised Auntie.

"You're a very attractive woman, Valerie," Cody volunteered. "I guess I shouldn't be surprised in view of Nicole's dynamite looks."

"How sweet," Auntie gushed. "Thank you, Cody."

"How did you like the show last night?" Professor Reims inquired.

"Loved it," I replied enthusiastically. "I never laughed so hard."

"I never got so hard while laughing," Tommy added.

"Tommy, you're so gauche," Cody declared.

"Are all salespeople that way?"

"It's called hard sell, so I sell when I'm hard."

"Don't be a prick," Eric commented with no smile to lessen the impact.

"The women around here are practically naked," Tommy complained, "and I get criticized for being honest."

"Honestly obnoxious I'd say," Eric countered.

It was obvious that Tommy's constant pursuit of Cody was beginning to get to Eric. Normally the advances of others didn't bother him—he was one of the handsomest boys to ever visit the school, and now, as a young man, maturity had only increased his attractiveness—but Tommy Riddle was a peskily persistent sort who seemingly could not be deterred or embarrassed.

Claude Reims, always a popular professor, stepped in to defuse the dialogue. "The treasure hunt is almost ready to start. Why don't we all go to the athletic field together?"

"What are we supposed to be searching for?" I inquired.

"An antique dildo donated by the anthropology department."

"What good will that do me?" Tommy asked with a shrug.

"You can use it to cork your mouth," Eric replied.

"On second thought, maybe we should all go separately," Professor Reims said.

"I'll be quiet," Tommy promised, sensing correctly that he was at least partially at fault.

"That'll be a novelty," Eric sneered.

"Shhhh!" Cody admonished him, finger crossing her lips.

Professor Reims threw up his arms in a gesture of resignation and frustration. "It was easier handling just the girls alone," he confided to Aunt

Val. "I just sent them to the headmaster for disciplining, and that was that."

"What do you teach, Professor Reims?"

"Geography."

"How interesting," Aunt Valerie commented.

"The way he taught it it was," I confirmed. "Peninsulas were penises, mountains were tits, valleys were vaginas, lakes were pussy puddles, oases were belly buttons in the desert, geysers were assholes letting off steam—God, I can't remember all the colorful ways Professor Claude had of describing things."

"Fascinating," Aunt Val reacted. "I've often envied Nicole her Dumont education."

"It's about as liberal as one can get," Professor Reims acknowledged with an impish smile. "You'd do very well as a depiction of the topography of the Alps or the Himalayas."

"She alaya, too," I punned.

"Hima?" Aunt Val went along with the gag, pointing at the professor. "Sure I would."

"Don't tantalize a tutor of topography!"

"Lay a hand on those full moons to the bottom rear, Professor," I encouraged him.

"The Pyrenees just above the knees?" he asked with amusement.

"They won't bite," Auntie assured him, striking a provocative, ass-exaggerated pose.

Her almost bare buttocks proved irresistible to the professor. His eager hands held them like ripe melons as she pressed herself into his palms.

"Asstronomical!" he declared.

"Why don't we skip the treasure hunt and go looking for other treasures in the immediate vicinity of your hands?" Aunt Val suggested in her sultriest voice.

"Give me time to get a grip on myself," Professor Reims joked lamely. His cock had already given him away via its bobbing eagerness inside his slacks.

"I'd like a hand in helping you," Auntie responded, openly grabbing his rampant prick through the fabric.

The three of us had fallen back several steps from the others. They hardly noticed as Aunt Val and Claude disappeared into the hedges along the path. I moved up next to Cody as nonchalantly as I could.

"Where'd the prof go?" she asked, looking around in back of her.

"Oh," I fumbled for an excuse, "he wanted to show Aunt Val something in his office."

"I can imagine!" she replied, lifting her eyebrows.

"You always think the worst right away," Eric accused her.

"No," she responded immediately, "the best."

We spent the next two hours scouring the campus for the hidden dildo, made from a hippopotamus tusk. It was finally found by Simone Breton, who promptly christened it in her cunt. Another dance and cocktail party followed in the gym. I didn't get back to the cottage until almost four A.M. Aunt Val had not shown up at the dance at all, nor, for that matter, had Professor Reims. When I got to our room, she was fast asleep and unwakable. But in the morning she would not shut up, chattering like a magpie as I struggled to sleep.

"Geographically speaking," she buzzed in my ear, "Claude took your aunt on a trip around the world. Honey baby, I was never so gloriously cunt-fucked, ass-fucked, tit-fucked and mouth-fucked in my lyrical life. Oh, it was lovely, lovely, lovely!"

In my semi-stupor I wondered where this might lead in inspiring impressionable Aunt Valerie on another far-flung, farfetched crusade. Mulling that, I was gratefully swept into a sea of slumber which drowned out the sound of her voice and sent me far beyond the horizon of consciousness for hours and hours and hours.

chapter sixteen

As the countdown to conclusion began on Friday, the reunion action grew increasingly abandoned and accelerated. Copulation abounded indoors and out with markedly less reserve and restraint. Dr. Lucas Montaigne went about counseling the erotically entangled, declaring the passionate pairs "temporarily wedlocked" and anointing them with water from Lovers' Lake, a favorite student trysting spot near the campus. The curly cornsilk of my cunt was cultivated and harvested by reapers of both sexes and in the process I found myself jeweled with Dr. Luke's holy aqua more than just once or twice.

Dr. Duncan was more discreet in his dunking, cornering me in his office where he read from Chaucer's *The Canterbury Tales* while rocking on the fulcrum of my pussy. The "thees" and the "thous" were abundant as he praised the noble character of my cunt, as he termed it. My response was simply orgasmic, coming in grunts and groans as my favorite prof plowed the pasture of my pubes.

It was all headlong and nonstop, with sleep having to ambush most of the participants rather than being welcomed. Not everyone led the life I did beyond this celebration, and consequently they were even more reluctant than I to miss even a single second of the sizzling scenario.

"Sleep and Sex Experiments in Psychology Department Midnight Friday," the daily program announced. It offered the first potential opportunity to treat the clashing forces of exhaustion and eroticism in one fell swoop, and as a result, the turnout was sizable despite the late hour.

Dr. Henri Chartres was head of the department and its most distinguished researcher. He was a slim, furtive man of serious mien with a habit of licking his lips as he spoke. It made his words seem delicious, and for that reason, I had always enjoyed his classes. He seemed particularly edgy and excited as we filed into the lab at midnight.

"Which of you will it be at this witching hour?" he inquired, forcing a quick, nervous laugh.

Most of the lab tables had been topped with mattresses for the occasion, making the long, narrow room resemble a dormitory with high beds. At the head of each table rested an electronic monitoring device with dangling wires waiting to be taped to the erogenous zones of volunteers. Dr. Chartres's beady eyes darted about sizing up prospects.

"The purpose of this reunion research is opportunistically twofold," he began in earnest the moment everyone was inside and seated, "seeking to study male sexual erections of guests and faculty alike while in a soporific state and—for the first time anywhere—the effect of oral stimulation on the length and frequency of tumescence . . . "

"Is he trying to give us guests a hard time?" Jeff Whittaker quipped from the chair next to me.

Aunt Val sat on the other side of me, absolutely entranced by the idea of advancing higher education through a series of erections.

"Isn't this marvelous?" she said, her eyes wide and vividly alive.

"You've probably already done enough lay research to qualify for credits in this course," I kidded her.

"This is serious," she sniffed. "Pay attention."

Dr. Chartres continued, "A normal man spends one and a half to two hours in a tumescent state while asleep, enjoying three to four erections a night."

"How can he enjoy them if he's asleep?" Eric Blye interrupted.

"I meant 'enjoy' in the sense of good health," Dr. Henri explained with just a hint of impatience. "In youth they would find fuller expression in seminal emissions . . ."

"Wet dreams?" I suggested in more basic language.

"If you prefer, Nicole."

"*I'd* prefer not to have the seeds wasted like that."

"Nicole!" Aunt Val reprimanded. "Please allow the doctor to continue."

"My apologies, Dr. Chartres," I said.

"No apologies necessary. I enjoy discussion. You have a good head on your shoulders, and you should use it."

"To give head," a male voice shouted.

"Yea!" a chorus of other masculine voices seconded the notion.

The group obviously had a short attention span after day-long partying. It would be wise for Dr. Chartres to get on with the experiments in short order before the audience got too restless to attain the necessary sleep-inducing relaxation.

"Boys," he addressed the visiting young men demeaningly, "please strip at least from the waist down, but preferably to total nakedness and then mount the mattresses assembled in the room . . . "

"You mean fuck the feathers?" a semi-smashed jester asked.

"Place yourselves supinely upon them," Dr. Chartres specified with a small sigh of exasperation. "My assistants will then attach the monitoring devices to your flesh, after which the lights will be dimmed and suitably somnolent music will be piped into the room until all of the male participants are asleep . . . "

All of the men elected to strip completely, creating a forest of cocks rising from the plateaus of multiple abdomens. A few were semi-hard due to the circumstances of exhibitionism and the presence of so many attractive female fellatio volunteers.

"The Great Sleep Suck-off," promotion-minded Tommy Riddle declared as he closed his eyes and gave a fond pat to his prick.

In a matter of minutes, every man present was wired and racked, earphones over his ears and a soft mask over his eyes. Dr. Chartres—or Dr. Henri, as most of us preferred to address him— held his index finger to his lips to encourage the women present to remain silent. It took surprisingly little time to transport all of the men into the arms of Morpheus.

"Be patient," Dr. Henri whispered to us. "The erections must occur naturally, without any outside stimulation, in order to validate the experiment."

We sat beside the table-beds like a corps of fellatio Florence Nightingales watching over a field of flaccid cocks, waiting for them to grow.

"Isn't that a beauty?" Aunt Val singled out one plump specimen.

It lay there on the belly of an athletically built young man like a hairless mink, smooth and sleek, with a pair of plum-sized balls tossed in a hairy sac over one thick thigh. We both watched as he unconsciously fondled what must have been his favorite toy, encouraging it to swell ever so slightly almost from the beginning of his slumber.

"Let's bet on which one gets hard first," Simone Breton suggested in a hushed voice.

"How much?" I asked.

"A magnum of the best champagne the village vintner has in stock.

"You've got a deal," I agreed.

All the other girls joined in, including Aunt Val. The contest helped pass the time and gave the proceedings something of the air of a cockfight. Dr. Chartres seemed not to mind so long as we kept reasonably quiet and remained ready to lick the lobs as they rose to glory.

As luck would have it, Aunt Val's chosen cock fattened first for the kill, looking like the clenched fist and forearm of an athlete as it trembled to total tumidity. She did not pause to savor victory, however, bending immediately to the task of tonguing the head and neck of the victorious prick.

"Lick it, don't swallow it," someone told her.

She was so voracious in the art of sucking it did sometimes appear that she intended to devour cock or cunt totally. Dr. Henri slipped up next to her and watched intently, stopwatch in hand.

"Keep it up indefinitely," he encouraged her. "My object is to determine if man can remain tumescent and yet asleep over a prolonged period of time without losing rigidity or ejaculating."

"A noble cause," Cody Cameron commented rather facetiously.

"A no-bull cause, too," I punned. "No real bull would stand for being coaxed without coming."

By this time, other phallic monuments were rising around the room, each greeted with lip service from female classmates. I went down on one nearby tower, watching the eyelids of my victim for any signs of fluttering and emerging consciousness. He stayed firm for about five or six minutes, but then softened despite my manipulative mouth. Dr. Henri dutifully recorded the results in his notebook and directed me to another upright organ several tables down.

No one proved able to maintain an erection for any great length of time without awakening the recipient of the oral massage. It was fun, however, watching the cocks rise and retreat several times over the course of the night. By dawn the room began to resemble a blizzard as come flew like snowflakes from the awakening penises and their attached individuals.

Aunt Val was a child in a snowstorm as she wandered about tasting the various flavors and consistencies of come available in the lab from sunrise onward.

"Caviar, caviar," she proclaimed happily as she dabbled in the little pools of sperm fish.

Dr. Chartres called an end to the experiment shortly before nine A.M. when it threatened to run into the last full day's program of activities. The homecoming reunion was due to end on noon Sunday, with a final convocation in the school auditorium.

"I wish to thank all of you for your splendid cooperation, particularly those of you who are the guests of our beloved alumnae," he said in concluding the test. "We of the Académie Dumont have always been leaders in all we undertake, and this experiment in erectile limitations and potential is in that great tradition of academic pioneering. When I present my paper on this noble project to the international body of scholars, you may be assured it will be dedicated to these brilliant members of the alumnae and their generous guests, namely each and every one of you. Thank you again—and may you enjoy to the fullest every remaining moment of this tremendous reunion celebration . . ."

We filed out with a sense of achievement, the satisfaction of having done something eminently worthwhile in the midst of our bacchanal.

"If my days are numbered," Aunt Valerie declared as we emerged into the morning sun, "I hope they're all number sixty-nine."

It was a sentiment shared by all as we proceeded en masse to the morning champagne brunch kicking off our final full day at Dumont.

chapter seventeen

To the surprise of all of us, the only female non-graduate present—Aunt Valerie—was summoned shortly after noon to the offices of the head-master, Dr. Marcel Beauregard.

"What the hell does your headmaster Bozo want with her?" Tommy Riddle asked on behalf of all.

"Maybe she's getting an honorary diploma," Eric Blye conjectured. "She sucks and fucks like an alumna."

"Since really getting to know him for the first time at this reunion," Cody said, "I'd be inclined to think his motives are less honorable than that. Your aunt is a real sexual knockout."

"Thanks, Cody," I replied in Aunt Val's behalf. "She'd really appreciate that coming from a younger version of the same thing."

"What is this," Tommy asked, "a mutual masturbation society?"

"Do you have anything against that?" I challenged.

"Only that nobody's hand is on my gland," he replied breezily.

"You may be right, Cody," I returned to her speculation. "Bozo might have erotic designs on her."

"Painted with his cock," Eric quipped.

I shrugged. "She's old enough to cross or uncross her legs," I said. "He's not going to sail into her harbor like a full-masted schooner without a permit."

"Right now he's probably wailing 'thar she blows!' " Tommy declared.

"I don't think you're showing proper respect for either my aunt or Dr. Beauregard. Just to prove everything's on the up-and-up, I'm going over to the administration building and conduct my own investigation."

"A million francs says the only thing on the up-and-up there is Bozo's prick," Tommy proposed a bet.

My brief fit of pique passed, and my usual perspective returned. "You've got to lay me some very big odds if you want Auntie being laid."

"I wouldn't touch the whole bet with a ten-foot pole," Eric noted.

"If you had a ten-foot pole, you could touch any hole on earth," Cody cracked. "They'd be flocking to your doorstep."

"Probably flocking right *on* it," Tommy kidded.

"Ugh!" I grunted in mock disgust. "I'm leaving."

"We want a report on your spying," Eric called after me.

"Every flick of his prick," Simone added.

"Alas, my class has no class," I sighed in parting.

"Just ass," Simone called after me.

With those thoughts ringing in my ears, I hurried down the path to the main building several hundred yards away. I had played peeping Tom and eavesdropper there in the past and knew exactly where and how to hide to observe and overhear what went on in Dr. Beauregard's office. It made me feel like a precocious schoolgirl all over again as I parted the bushes and climbed the ledge adjacent to his offices.

I suppose I shouldn't have been surprised, but surprised I was to see Aunt Valerie standing naked over the equally nude body of Bozo slumped across his desk. In her hand was a large, thick paddle of some kind of dark hardwood, the handle clutched in her fist as if it were a cock she was jerking off. There were prominent scarlet blotches on the headmaster's bare buttocks, and Auntie seemed poised to deliver another smack to his plump cheeks.

"All right you sonofabitch," I heard her say with a theatrical snarl, "are you going to behave in the future, or do I crack your fucking ass again?"

Bozo's voice was weak and weepy. "I want for myself only what my bad students receive in punishment for their errant ways. I don't mean to do bad things—I just can't help myself."

The paddle swooshed through the air, landing with a flat, dull impact on the breadth of his butt. He cried out at first contact, then began whimpering as she poised for another assault.

"You cock-sucking hypocrite," Auntie enunciated with slow, distinct emphasis, "you deserve to be beaten until blood comes out of your asshole like come out of your cock . . . ''

"If I deserve it—do it," he pleaded, sobbing softly.

Once again Auntie swung, a beautiful arcing motion that sent the paddle's face flush against his posterior. His rump was now so red that it was difficult to determine whether it was merely temporarily bruised or actually bleeding. Dr. Beauregard wept openly now.

"I have been disobedient," he confessed tearfully. "You are right in punishing me for my sins."

"Suck my cunt!" Auntie demanded, strutting to the other side of the desk and pushing her pussy into his wet face.

"Gladly," he gasped before losing his lips and tongue in the abundance of her rich lode of labia.

As he slurped and licked and sucked with liquid abandon, Aunt Val repeatedly tapped his tush with the flat of the paddle. "You academic asshole," she sneered, "I ought to make you suck every cunt that ever graduated from this cheap fraud of a finishing school. You rotten, lying, faggot bastard sonofabitch!"

The more she demeaned and denounced him, the more hungrily he lapped at her lap. I might have stood a bit more but not much more, had I not slipped and fallen, my landing cushioned by the thick mesh of bushes surrounding the building. So that was Dr. Beauregard's private passion —being punished! It was quite a revelation to me considering how avidly he seemed to pursue the punishment of others.

I skipped a bawdy sing-along in the gym to return to my room for a brief nap. After all, we had been up all night participating in the psychology experiment, and my head was a bit heavy. But there was to be no rest for me. There, waiting in the parlor of the cottage, were—surprise of surprises—Count Erich and Countess Ulrica.

"Nicole, darling!" Ulrica cried as she hurried over to greet me. "We've missed you so, dear."

"Countess!" I cried out. "Erich! What an unexpected treat!"

"Hello, my love," the count responded, kissing me on the cheek not occupied by Ulrica.

"The reunion's almost over," I said. "Why didn't you come sooner?"

"Perhaps only a phase of it is over," Erich said with an air of mystery.

"Tomorrow noon is the finale," I reported. "Then it becomes just nostalgic history."

"Perhaps," Ulrica said as cryptically as her husband.

"Aunt Val is here. She's with the headmaster at the moment."

"No one is more the master in that department than she," the count observed impishly.

"Erich!" his wife reprimanded him. "This is Nicole's alma mater."

He looked away, showing not the slightest bit of remorse. There was no longing for discipline and obedience training in Count Erich von Hoffman.

"Tell me the real reason why you came," I asked Erich, certain something was being kept from me.

"At dinner tonight, Dr. Beauregard has given me the opportunity to make a brief speech."

"I never knew you to go in for oratory," I said with good-natured suspicion. "Oral sex, yes, but not oratory."

"Perhaps that's an undiscovered, hidden facet of my complex personality," he teased.

"Every facet of yours has been discovered and explored by Ulrica and me. Isn't that true, Ulrica?"

She smiled sweetly. "Wait until dinner, darling. It'll be more fun that way."

Reluctantly, with curiosity killing my pussy, I agreed.

The last full dinner of reunion week was a feast that would have gladdened a glutton's heart and gorged his stomach. In order to accommodate the crowd and the huge pyramids of fruits, vegetables and cheeses along with mountains of breads, meats and pastries atop the tables, the affair was held in the school gymnasium. It was elaborately decorated with bunting, flags, streamers, and balloons, along with thousands of white flowers.

It was akin to a buffet, but with each of the rows of tables laden with its own selection of appetizers and entrées. The uniformed waiters limited their service to cocktails and other beverages, making certain that glasses were always full.

I sat between the count and countess, both of whom had hearty appetites for virtually everything, particularly the large selection of wines from France and Germany. The gusto with which they enjoyed good food and drink reflected their basically rural background, luxurious as it was.

"The way to a man's heart is through his stomach," the count recited an old adage.

"And the way to his libido?" I questioned over a serving of escargots.

Erich's eyes twinkled. "Through his penile protuberance, of course."

"Have you ever eaten penis?" Aunt Valerie asked from across the table.

"Literally?"

"Yes. The organ of reproduction."

"Woodcock, bantam cock, yes," Erich responded, "but actually masticate a male cock, no."

"I have," Aunt Val said. "I ate roast wild boar cock in Texas once and barbecued reindeer penises in an Alaskan Eskimo village."

"Well, suck my salamander," the count smiled. "That is fellatio carried to the nth degree."

"I much prefer confining my consumption to extracting the sap from the trunk," Ulrica commented merrily.

"Come, come," I kidded, "let's elevate this conversation above the crotch."

"What are you suddenly getting crotchety about?" Auntie asked.

I chose to ignore her question, recognizing it as her limp play on words. Aunt Val was no match for her slogan writers, yet she continually attempted to top them as well as me.

"By the way," I changed the subject, "how did your meeting with Dr. Beauregard go this afternoon?"

"Spankingly," she replied, smiling smugly.

"Is that open to Freudian interpretations?" I queried.

"As open as my legs at an orgy," she answered, obviously pleased by her own glibness.

"You mean you applied your palm to his posterior?"

"I spanked his ass. Does that answer your question?"

The count and countess followed our banter back and forth like spectators at a tennis match, their eyes moving while their lips remained silent.

"Partly," I conceded. "But you've aroused my curiosity, Aunt Val. Are you implying that dear Dr. Beau is into obedience disciplining?"

"He loves it," she confirmed.

"I find that hard to believe," I lied.

"If you saw how hard it made him, you'd believe."

"*Administering* discipline is his thing," I continued, "or so I always thought."

"That's the reason he wants to be punished," she explained, sinking her teeth into a breast of capon.

"Guilt?"

She shrugged. "Probably," she replied. "But I think it goes much deeper than that. Maybe his mother spanked him when she caught him playing with himself, and now he associates coming with whipping."

"Did you produce any whipped cream?" I asked.

"It seemed like a quart. I never saw anybody come so much. It was like milking a cow."

Aunt Val's eyes shifted to the center of the head table where Dr. Beauregard sat. Those of the count, countess, and myself followed suit.

"Look at him," she said with just the slightest hint of disdain, "so prim, so proper, so pristine. Isn't it remarkable how sexually deceptive people can be?"

"We're all animals when it comes to coming," Countess Ulrica said.

"Not I," the count disagreed. "I have a halo around the head of my cock."

"A romantic delusion," his wife retorted. "It's just scored foreskin, that's all. Nothing angelic."

"It feels heavenly," I sided with Erich for fun.

"Thank you, dear Nicole," he replied. "You've warmed the cockles of my cock."

"No more than I warmed the bottom of Bozo this afternoon," Aunt Val injected.

Ulrica frowned prettily as she performed fellatio on a jumbo shrimp. "Idle chatter," she sniffed.

The repartee went into recess as we all concentrated on the splendid repast. The gourmet dishes were delicious beyond words, despite the rather informal manner of serving them. But the reunion committee had voted unanimously in favor of the family-style setup for the food service, preferring to concentrate the waiters' attention on the libations. As a result, almost everyone present was soon soaring.

As the evening progressed, toasts were offered to everything from Dr. Duncan's dong to Aunt Valerie's vagina. I almost let the pussy out of the bag when I proposed a tribute to Dr. Beauregard's buttocks. However, he countered quickly with a touching testimonial to my tits.

"The memory of your mammaries," he declared, "will linger long after this homecoming is gone and we are home coming alone."

I swam through a fiery brandied dessert and then devoted myself to champagne and cognac in alternating sips as Bozo again staggered to his feet to make an announcement.

"Lewdies and genitalmen," he punned with a tilted grin on his flushed face, "may I have your undivided attention from your divided legs, please? We have the great honor to have in our midst this momentous evening the distinguished Count Erich von Hoffman of Austria and his lovely chatelaine, the Countess Ulrica. I know you are going to be intrigued and enchanted by what he has to say to all of you. It is my distinct pleasure now to introduce to you Count Erich, to whom we already owe a lasting debt of gratitude for having sponsored the education of our gorgeous alumna Nicole at the Académie Dumont . . ."

Whistles and applause greeted Dr. Beau's comments and introduction. Count Erich rose, beaming like a formally attired Santa Claus. He held out his hands in a quest for quiet and the crowd responded with a chant: "Nicole! Nicole! Nicole!"

I got up at the count's insistence, acknowledging the cheers with a deep, tit-revealing bow. Another outburst resulted before the clapping and hooting finally subsided.

"Dear friends at Académie Dumont," Erich began, "the countess and I wish first of all to thank you profusely for your kindness and hospitality on so many past occasions. Now we are in your debt even more after this marvelous banquet and the camaraderie you've shown toward us this wonderful evening. It is not only inspirational, but deeply moving as well. Perhaps that will begin to explain why I am motivated emotionally to attempt to extend this festive celebration beyond its official conclusion tomorrow noon . . . "

Even those blurred by imbibing seemed to sense something dramatic was about to be revealed. The crowd stirred and only the tinkling of ice in glasses could be heard after the count cleared his throat before continuing.

"As a special tribute to all of you who have graduated from Académie Dumont, their friends and guests, as well as those who taught you so well, I should like at this time to extend an invitation to one and all to join Countess Ulrica, Nicole, her Aunt Valerie, and myself on a grand voyage of nearly two thousand miles over the course of the Danube River from southwestern Germany through Austria, Czechoslavakia, and Hungary—ending appropriately in the Paris of Eastern Europe, Budapest . . . "

Pandemonium interrupted Count Erich's invitation. The ensuing bedlam proclaimed that no one present had really wanted the partying to end —at least not yet. Now here was dear, sweet Erich offering a magnificent opportunity, a grandiose solution to the dilemma of a premature climax to a reunion that clearly was eager to go on.

"I love you!" I cried out as I looped my arms about the count and kissed him repeatedly on his glowing cheeks. "You couldn't have given me and all the rest of us a more wonderful present, you darling devil!"

Countess Ulrica remained seated, smiling through a shower of kisses from dozens of alumnae who milled about, laughing and crying, pinching themselves to assure themselves it was all really real.

"I don't know whether I can come," Aunt Valerie lamented amidst the happy throng.

"You can come, you *will* come!" I insisted over the noisy celebration.

She looked at me and then suddenly hugged me tightly. "You're right!"

chapter eighteen

Not one of the reunion revelers declined Count Erich's invitation. In fact, the crowd boarding the chartered steamer swelled from the homecoming total as graduates sent for family members to join the cruise. Even Dr. Beauregard cast aside his academic mien and assumed the casual, carefree composure of the majority of passengers aboard the S.S. *Johann Sebastian*. I was surprised and amused to encounter him hours before sailing time clad in plaid Bermuda shorts and a scarlet-striped rugby shirt.

"Dr. Beau," I exclaimed, using the shortened version of his name favored—along with "Bozo" —by students and faculty alike behind his back, "I never knew you had such pretty dimpled knees."

"I have other attractive components and orifices as well," he responded with a rare smile.

"You mean there's fizz in your physiology?"

"Yes, and life in my libido."

"That I believe," I agreed. "You should get plenty of exercise before we reach Budapest."

"I'm Hungary for it," he punned.

Count Erich, who was standing at the rail nearby observing his guests arrive, at first did not recognize the headmaster in such sporty garb. When his identity did become clear to him, he expressed the same surprise I'd felt earlier.

"I never knew Dr. Beauregard to be without a shirt and tie," he noted.

Aunt Valerie laughed. "You should come with me sometime."

"If he keeps sucking on that champagne bottle in his hand," I commented, "he'll be tying one on in no time."

"I thought he was a teetotaler," Countess Ulrica said.

"More like a tit-totaler the way his eyes are sizing up all the women," I joked.

"He doesn't miss anything about any of the misses," Auntie agreed.

"I think he needs a good spanking," I suggested.

"He'd probably enjoy a good licking," Aunt Val agreed.

"I hope Dr. Beauregard wasn't held in such light regard when you were a student here, Nicole," Ulrica said.

"Bozo? We hardly saw him at all on campus. All the administration crap came through Dean Torrance."

"Poor Dean!" the countess lamented. "He's the only faculty member who couldn't make the reunion or the trip."

"I understand he tried to arrange an earlier parole," I responded, "but the authorities said no."

"What a shame," Ulrica commented. "And all

he did was help a poor young woman who complained to him that she couldn't get herself molested."

"So he molested her to restore her faith in herself," Aunt Valerie reflected playfully.

"It was the humane thing to do," Ulrica declared. "After all, she was not a baby."

"Only a virgin," I noted jestingly.

"I'm serious," the countess said.

"So am I."

"That could never be the case with you and Gilda," Aunt Val stated. "I mean, being cherry after eighteen."

"You're telling tales out of school," I accused her playfully.

"I wouldn't be surprised if you were selling tail in school," she retaliated with a half-smile.

"Don't think our enterprising little senior-class minds didn't toy with the idea," I confessed.

"Speaking of Gilda," the countess said, "where do you suppose she is at this very moment?"

"Confined to some psycho ward with an acute jealous fit," I suggested.

"Don't be so harsh on her, Nicole," Ulrica pleaded. "You two have had such a lovely, lasting friendship over the years. A little misunderstanding shouldn't be allowed to undermine it in any way."

"She's always been as green as her eyes over everything good that happens to me," I declared. "I never get that way about her."

"Nicole," the countess said warmly, "you are a challenge to every woman alive with your extreme beauty and sensuality. You must understand that not everyone can cope with that."

"But Gilda is no slouch when it comes to sexy looks. We go along for months at times with no dissension whatsoever. But then—zap!—she suddenly blows her top when she should be blowing somebody's bottom. I get disgusted with her pettiness at those times.''

"I'm sure she's sorry, missing half of the re-union and now the boat trip as well," the countess said.

"Fuck her," I replied calmly.

"I'd like to," Aunt Val chimed in lightly. "Where can I find her?"

"The last anybody heard, she was in Rio with her playboy millionaire," I said. "Who knows where they are by now?"

Count Erich, who'd been listening to the conversation without comment, suggested we all go to the upper deck where a gala bon-voyage party was about to begin.

"The band's all set to start," he announced. "I want a real Académie Dumont sendoff for the trip.''

After a week of partying together, almost all the faces were familiar, if not all the names. There had been name tags on each at one time but in the course of multiple sheddings of clothes and inhibitions most of them had either disappeared or shown up on the wrong people. Consequently, everyone was addressed as "honey" or "baby" or "darling"—along with riper and more lurid monickers as well—much of the time. "Bitch" and "bastard" were a pair of latter favorites, along with "prick" and "pussy."

I liked being addressed as "Nicole pussy," a fondness which spread rapidly once I had confessed it to a partner in copulation.

The upper deck was alive with decorations and people as well as an eighteen-piece orchestra. The count gave the opening downbeat, and instantly the afternoon air was rife with rhythm. I let myself be swept into the swirl of bodies by René Tremain, who had seemed to be ignoring me since Gilda's departure. He certainly wasn't doing it any longer; he pressed his prominent prick deeply into the flesh of my groin as we danced so closely together that I could feel the texture of his pores against my face.

"You dance divinely, monsieur," I said as we spun over the hardwood deck.

"Your body is an inspiration," he replied in a resonant voice. "It sets all of my flesh dancing."

"I know. I can feel the throb of your baton."

"I hope that you will find time for waltzing horizontally with me on the blue Danube," he said in a hoarse whisper laced with lust.

"I'm smiling vertically at your suggestion."

"A lovely smile it is, too," he replied. "I was privileged to be on the speaker's platform during Dr. Beau's opening remarks."

"Aha!" I cried out. "You caught our flash of gash—which was intended only for the eyes of Dr. Beau."

"Such a swarm of curls," he reminisced fervently, "as thick as bees around a hive. They were meant for more than a single pair of eyes to enjoy."

"Apparently you found the crop of the girl next to me more to your liking," I said with an air of mild indignation.

"Oh, no," he protested. "It's just that she had made herself so readily and relentlessly available, that's all. My heart and my hard long to be part of you, Nicole pussy."

"René," I teased him, "don't be a fickle fucker. The girl with autumn in her womb has spring in her legs just for you."

"Ha!" he laughed hollowly. "Before a cock crows twice, she's down thrice—regardless who stands behind it."

"You find her promiscuous?" I baited him for my own amusement.

"I find her not only promiscuous, but delicious as well."

"There's a lot of promise in promiscuity," I philosophized. "If you recall, my graduating class's motto was 'Prosperity, Polygamy, and Promiscuity."

"You're as clever as you are cute," he responded, his cock planted firmly against the cage of my cunt.

"And you're as hard as you are handsome," I replied.

"What stateroom are you in?"

"I'm on deck at the moment."

"You won't tell me?" he questioned, sounding disappointed.

I smiled at his frustration. "I don't know yet," I reported. "The count made the arrangements, and I haven't asked him yet."

"I'm in 209. Do you suppose you could visit me there after the party?"

"Will you be capable of a fitting salute by then?" I asked coyly.

"My tongue never sleeps."

"How about Peter Dickie?" I inquired.

"He's so wide awake right now, he might be exhausted by then," he answered honestly.

"See if you can keep him up. I wouldn't want him to miss anything."

The music stopped and I turned away, leaving René exposed with a prominent erection. He immediately doubled over and feigned a seizure.

"Is he all right?" the girl next to me asked. "He looks like he's having a stroke."

"That's what he needs," I suggested. "A good stroking."

Before she could react to my remark, I disappeared into the crowd. Everyone who hadn't been dancing seemed clustered about a long bar staffed by half a dozen mixologists. I headed there, too.

"Nicole!" a familiar voice called out. "You elusive little bitch, hold still for a moment so I can grab you!"

My eyes skipped over the bobbing heads in search of my pursuer.

"Charles!" I shouted when my gaze met his. "What a marvelous surprise!"

It was Charles Leroux, my novelist friend from the Riviera. His book, *The Adultery Commitment,* was a current best-seller, and the rumors persisted that it was based in part on my life. I was seemingly alone in accepting his word that it was not.

"Whatever brings you here?" I asked when he was able to ford his way through the throng to my side.

"What else, but to have sex with you."

"How sweet!" I gushed. "But how did you know?"

"You've been so busy being a part of it that you're probably unaware that your school reunion —and now this boat trip—are the scandal of the year on the Continent," he informed me. "The media has been absolutely masturbating itself with pictures and stories of all the alleged indiscretions taking place."

"Nothing derogatory to Dumont, I hope?"

Charles laughed. "They'll probably be flooded with enrollment applications from all over the world," he predicted.

"It has been a juicy jamboree, I must admit."

"That's why I couldn't resist calling Count Erich and begging for an invitation. He was most gracious about it."

"Nobody likes a party more than Erich," I

agreed. "But tell me about yourself—how's the book doing?"

"Well, the book that is *not* about Nicole is doing just sensationally. I'm right in the midst of getting an American publishing offer for it."

"Great! At last you'll be as famous as you deserve to be."

"More likely infamous," he replied. "I have two paternity suits pending already—the greedy little bitches."

"You've always told everyone you'd had a vasectomy."

He smiled mischievously. "Never trust a writer of fiction. Truth is alien to all of them."

"Devil!" I accused him. "It's a good thing none of your little fishes hatched in my hatchery, you deceitful bastard."

"I'm careful, darling. I'd feel guilty all my life if ever I contributed even the faintest stretch mark to your awesome anatomy."

"If bullshit were beans, Charles, you'd be the mayor of Boston."

"If you're implying that I'm half-baked, may I cook for a while in the oven of your ovaries?"

"I have a prior reservation for the space," I told him. "You'll have to take a number and wait to be called."

"Sixty-nine!"

I pushed him away playfully. "Go get drunk. I hardly know you sober."

"You *will* call when there's an opening in your opening?"

"I'll wave my legs—wide," I kidded him.

I watched as he inserted himself into the crowd, swiveling his way to the busy bar. God, it would be fun having him on the cruise—even if he did take notes for some future novel. I looked about and saw René hurrying toward the passageway leading to his cabin. Perhaps he was undergoing an erotic emergency. The Good Samaritan in me dictated that I follow and relieve the pressure in his pubes. I decided I could forgo a few minutes of the party to participate in a bit of humane fucking.

"Nicole!" Cody Cameron called out.

"Right back!"

"Nicole!" Jeff Whittaker shouted.

"Be with you in a minute."

"Nicole!" Tommy Riddle exclaimed, grabbing futilely at my arm in passing.

"Later."

It wasn't easy escaping everyone for the sake of a little poetic licentiousness. But the idea of scoring with Monsieur Tremain had grown considerably more attractive with each glass of champagne I imbibed. Dr. Duncan would not like it, nor would a certain young lady who was among the missing—two factors which made fucking him all the more intriguing.

I slipped down the staircase to the middle deck and then watched as the numbers declined from 250 down to 209. With clenched fist, I rapped my knuckles twice against the door. The sound of muffled voices and then sensuous giggling greeted my knocking.

"Who is it?" René's voice inquired anxiously.

"Open up, you horny bastard," I replied.

The door moved just enough to permit a sliver of light to penetrate.

"Nicole!" he gasped—an odd reaction, I thought.

"What's the matter?" I demanded.

"I—I—" he stammered.

I threw myself against the door, knocking him aside. Then time seemed to freeze for a split-second, as though the scene had been caught in a photograph. It seemed an eternity before I was able to comprehend what I saw. Then I fell back and drew the door closed behind me. It was hard to believe but my eyes did not lie. There on the bed, in all her naked glory, had been not the most unlikely but certainly the most unexpected femme fatale of all—Gilda Morrow!

chapter nineteen

Forgive and forget. Suck and fuck. These were the credos adopted by Gilda and me in our rapid and rapturous reconciliation.

She cried when she came—tears of joy and passion made all the sweeter by the extraction of bitterness. The soft seashell of her snatch was never more enthralling, never more pungently palatable. I licked her labia ardently and combed my fingers through the wool of her womb while she performed similar rites in the chapel of my cunt. We had always had a marvelous sexual compatibility, one which somehow seemed to be enhanced by periods of estrangement. I came like a roller coaster, with enormous, spellbinding ups and thrilling, breathtaking plunges downward. It was all too wonderful to last but we did our best to sustain the exhilaration as long as possible, remaining mute in the muffs of one another until all hope for yet another climax had to be abandoned.

"Darling dearest," Gilda whispered as she cradled my face in her hands, "let's never part again for any reason whatever."

"Never," I agreed breathlessly.

"I want you to have René as a token of our enduring love," she surprised me by saying.

"Then you must have Roderick."

"I love you," she sighed.

We kissed tenderly, our nipples and pussies meeting simultaneously. For a moment it was as though we were one, a single heart beating, one source of blood for both, a shared passion to motivate us. Love was generosity, and here we were offering our favorite faculty lovers to one another. A great surge of affection coursed through my veins with that realization.

"I want to put Dr. Duncan in you," I declared softly.

"Then I want to do the same for you with René," she replied.

"Side by side?"

"Together always."

We kissed again and then set about to arrange the crossover of cocks. The two men were surprised, to say the least, but more than willing to participate in our solidarity ritual. I suspected they'd both harbored secret designs on us, restraining themselves only through fears of wrath and reprisal. What could be lovelier than to have us not only condone such seductions, but to physically assist in carrying them out?

"Thou taketh my phallic adornment in thine hands to deliver it unto the cathedral of St. Gilda the Divine?" Dr. Duncan recited as the magic moment arrived. "Pray, place it gently in the pew of her pubes that I might savor its succulence and anoint it with the oil of my organ . . ."

157

"Do you always talk like that even when you fuck?" Gilda inquired bluntly.

"Only the act of cunnilingus stills my tongue in speech," he replied, boring his rosy prick into the dense forest of her crotch.

"René," Gilda motioned to Monsieur Tremain as he stood watching her being fucked, "let me introduce your cock to Nicole's cunt."

"I thought you'd never ask," he responded more lightly than his swollen penis indicated his true mood.

"I'm a very wholesome girl," I set up a potential straight line.

"I can tell." He took the bait. "You've got some hole!"

Gilda grabbed a fat fistful of pure prick and brushed it against the springy cornsilk curls of my cunt. It tickled in a compellingly carnal sort of way. I could feel the tissues of my twat pucker as though trying to suck in the burgundy head of his cock.

"Let's fuck," I urged.

Her fingers spread the petals of my pussy like a blossom. It took only a slight push from René to penetrate the outer layer of cunt flesh. Gilda then slapped him sharply across the cheeks of his ass, driving his tool all the way into me in one dramatic plunge.

"Ooooooh!" I exhaled in erotic ecstasy.

"He fucketh thee, Nicole," Roderick observed, appearing more than content with his change of cunt.

"You faculty fuckers are something else," I declared, wedging myself against the bulkhead to keep from being driven from the bed.

"Play with his balls," Gilda advised me. "It gives his cock convulsions."

I did as she instructed, and sure enough, his

prick jerked spastically with each squeeze.

"Easy," René requested, "or else I'll come prematurely."

"Easy come, easy blow," I said in reply. "If that happens, you'll just have to face it."

"A tempting proposition," he replied. "I look forward to sucking you, Nicole."

"A fast come means lickety-split," I jested.

Gilda was quiet now except for heavy breathing, a sure sign she was en route to a massive orgasm. I decided to *cunt*centrate, too, and leave the bantering to prick and pussy.

"Your cunt sets up a marvelous suction," René reported in staccato fashion. "It seems to be pulling the come right out of me."

"You're ready to pop?" I asked.

"Almost," he winced.

"Flood me!"

He rose and fell like a derrick in the desert probing for oil. I tightened my haunches and wrapped my legs around his buttocks. The added pressure made his striving more difficult, but obviously also more delightful.

"You're a tight cunt," he gasped, perspiration beginning to jewel his brow.

"The better to strangle your fucking prick."

Gilda groaned as though mortally wounded, her body shuddering from a succession of overlapping climaxes. I clutched at her hand to capture a portion of the sweet shock waves surging through her system. Rod pulled out of her, dripping with come, and stuck his wet prick into the clasp of our hands as though it were a fresh cunt.

"You handsome hand-fucker," I managed to utter just before succumbing to my own orgasmic monsoon.

"Now!" René declared in a shout.

Come surfed from the crown of his cock,

through my golden curls onto the tanned plateau of my belly. There it gathered in small, lustrous oases as I weathered the storm of climaxes punishing my interior.

"Thou hast cast thine pearls before her," Dr. Duncan observed with apparent satisfaction over the performance of his colleague.

"Silence!" Gilda commanded. "Settle down and suck."

The Elizabethan tongue surrendered willingly, obligingly turning upside-down so that Gilda could communicate through his cock. Any desire not to be imitators was overcome by the desire to come in the same fashion. René and I settled easily into a wet and wonderful sixty-nine.

When we finally emerged from the cabin, the party was still in progress though considerably slowed down in numbers and spirit. Count Erich was still on his feet, though barely, while Aunt Valerie lay passed out on a chaise, a single red rose rising from her naked cunt.

We would be casting off somewhere in the night, but from the looks of things, only the captain and his crew would be around for the event. As for me, reunion with Gilda after reunion at Dumont was too much to handle without a good stretch of rest. I managed somehow to make it to my cabin—but from there on, Morpheus was the only witness to what happened next. By the time I returned to consciousness, we were passing the German town of Sigmaringen, well along on the first leg of our Danube journey.

chapter twenty

After the first day of leisurely cruising on the historic Danube, laced liberally with cocktails and canapés of every imaginable description, some very discernible patterns of pairings became obvious. There was something about the confinement of a ship, even a large one such as the S. S. *Johann Sebastian*, that discouraged random romances—at least outwardly. I never let any environment restrict my movements—or my morals, for that matter—but I did recognize that most people needed to identify specifically with someone else, even if only as a base from which to stray.

Recognizing this, I suppose I shouldn't have been surprised by one fairly frequent coupling; that of Aunt Valerie and my novelist friend Charles Leroux. They spent hours together on deck involved in what appeared to be deep, serious discussions. Since Auntie was hardly of any overwhelming intellectual depth I was naturally curious what the attraction was on Charles's part.

"He probably isn't trying to get into her head, he just likes the way she gives head," Gilda evaluated the situation for me.

That was suck-cinct but hardly satisfactory, from my point of view. Despite the fact that Aunt Val had technically been my guardian, I had always felt more like her protector than the reverse. She could be so gullible and then so generous because of that gullibility that I felt it my duty as her niece to shoo away as many of the charlatans who flocked to her as I possibly could. The lingering suspicion that perhaps he really had picked out pieces of my life to create his best-seller made me more than usually interested in what he was up to with Auntie.

As they waved to children on the shoreline, I sauntered over to where they were sitting. Aunt Val was wearing a provocatively plunging neckline and figure-hugging slacks that managed almost to detail the haired triangle of her crotch. Her labia lips were definitely visible, which no doubt accounted for Charles's positioning at her feet.

"My, you two are engrossed," I said casually as I pulled up a captain's chair next to them. "I hope I'm not intruding, but even if I am, I intend to remain because I haven't had a chance to talk to either of you since this voyage began."

"That is a mouthful," Charles responded, "and typically irrefutable."

"Refute all you like," I said, "but I will refuse your refutations."

"Your aunt is very charming," he declared smoothly. "I find her philanthropic activities most intriguing."

"She has more foundations going than a Manhattan building contractor," I noted.

"They're all so unique."

"Hey, Auntie," I jested. "That's one you haven't launched yet—a foundation for eunuchs."

"Now that would be really unique," Charles commented.

"It takes no balls at all," she quipped, surprising us both.

"You'll be doing your own slogans soon," I predicted.

"Nuts," she added with a straight face.

"Whatever you've been discussing with her, Charles," I noted, "you've certainly put a sharp edge on her repartee."

"She has a good head on her shoulders," he said.

"She gives good head on her shoulders, too."

"So I'm told," he replied.

"By whom, may I ask?" I questioned.

"By her," he retorted matter-of-factly.

"Auntie's no shrinking violet. She's more like a blooming magnolia."

"I'd like to do something with her one of these days," Charles confessed.

"I think her legs are open to suggestions," I joked.

"I meant in a professional sense."

"I don't think she takes money for it," I continued being facetious.

Charles sighed. "It was ever thus!"

"You're starting to talk like Dr. Duncan," I observed.

"Whoever he is."

"My favorite English professor."

"The one you were taking lessons from yesterday?" he asked slyly.

"English isn't his only tongue," I said coyly.

"I'm sure of that. At any rate, have you read the book yet?"

"Your book?"

"I said *the* book," he replied. "To what other could I possibly be referring?"

"You've added modesty to the virtues you lack, I see."

"One must be one's own drumbeater in the book business," he contended. "Otherwise one winds up in the back row on the bottom shelf."

"What does one do when one finds one's aunt going one-on-one with one's *romàn a clef*-palated friend?" I inquired with something akin to a smirk.

"Are you implying—?"

"I'm inquiring," I interrupted.

"Valerie's a very intriguing woman of depth and substance."

"As shallow as ebb tide at Mont St. Michel," I disagreed in a figurative way.

Auntie simply sat and watched, appearing not even to listen to our dialogue. She had the ability to fade out of conversations at will, concentrating all of her attention on other than the debate at hand. I could say virtually anything about her, be it derogatory or in praise, and there would be no reaction from her in the trance she was currently in.

"She's, well, different," he revised his appraisal.

"That I'll concede without question."

"She might form the outline for a character sometime," he admitted. "After all, writing is simply observing. All fictional beings have their roots in real-life individuals."

"You wouldn't be thinking of a whole book based on her, would you?"

"I met her for the first time only yesterday," he reminded me.

"You've been pumping her pretty thoroughly ever since, Charles."

"Psychologically, perhaps."

"And physiologically?" I probed.

He grinned in affirmation. "She's very versatile in vulval matters."

"So you've applied your double-edged sword to her."

"It's really quite blunt and cylindrical. If you like, I'll show it to you sometime."

Somehow I couldn't be angry with him, now or ever. He had the most beguiling way of worming himself out of situations. There was really little I could do to prevent him from using aspects of Auntie's life in a book, anyhow. So I did the only logical thing I could under the circumstances—I took him to my cabin, sucked his cock and fucked him, and added another spicy chapter to his life and mine.

chapter twenty-one

My concern over Aunt Valerie's involvement with
Charles Leroux might not have been unfounded,
but it certainly proved unnecessary. Before we had
even reached Regensburg, much less the Austrian
border, dear Auntie was pregnant with cause once
more.

"It came to me as I was coming," she revealed
with an air of mysticism. "I think that God com-
municates with mortals in the midst of orgasms."

If that were true, it meant He had lots of op-
portunities to get in touch with Aunt Val. On any
given day, she popped like popcorn over high
heat.

"You're not leaving the trip, are you?" I asked.

"Oh, but I must, dear child. My work comes
first."

"But you come more often."

"Be serious, Nicole. You can't go through life
being frivolous."

"The cause of the eunuchs finally got to you, huh?"

"No, no, no," she protested. "It's a much more universal matter than that. The plight of castrated men will have to wait."

"Dare I inquire what noble mission impels you to jump ship even before we reach Passau?"

"It's just now formulating in my brain. But essentially the concept is complete and the name decided upon."

"My breath is bated."

"As is your cunt."

"Auntie!" I exclaimed in feigned shock.

"The clit is like a worm attracting the sperm," she elaborated. "Hence the allusion."

"Lately everybody's talking like Dr. Duncan around here."

"Alas, dear Roderick, I knew him well," she continued her lighthearted banter.

"If I didn't know better, I'd swear you'd been drinking, Auntie."

"It's merely that I'm elated over being with cause again," she explained. "Prolonged partying without any purpose but pleasure is such an empty pursuit."

"I thought you'd at least stay with us until we reach the castle."

"No, child, I'm abandoning ship at the next port with rail connections. Then I'll catch a plane to Paris to get under way with my most important crusade yet."

"They're all your most important, until the next one comes along."

"Devotion is *de rigueur*," she insisted.

"Are you going to tell me, or do I have to guess?"

"I'm not evading your question, it's just that I

want you in the proper frame of mind and thinking in the correct context before revealing the nature of my newest mission.''

"Ejaculate it, please?"

"Your choice of verb is indicative of the general subject matter.''

"Come, come," I responded with a trace of exasperation.

Aunt Val looked at me with a quirky smile, apparently amused by my seeming impatience. All of her causes were *causes célèbres* as far as she was concerned and a bit of suspense in disclosing them only magnified their importance. At any rate, that was what she believed and practiced.

"I've told Count Erich about it, and he is most enthusiastic.''

"Insanity amuses him."

"Naughty but niece, Nicole," she reprimanded me mildly.

"All right then, don't tell me," I tried a new tack. "I'll see you when I get to Paris sometime in the next decade.''

Aunt Val laughed hollowly. "*Tantes* shouldn't taunt, should they?''

I shrugged and pouted.

"Dear, dear Nicole," she said softly, stroking my golden hair. "How I wish you'd come live with me and join me in my work.''

"Whatever it is," I responded.

She grew instantly serious. "Darling," she began emotionally, "God has chosen me once again to lead the way in an international campaign to educate people in the virtues of regular fornication. Everyone on earth should enjoy the benefits of intercourse on a daily basis. It's essential to good mental and physical health, regardless of age. Therefore, on behalf of the peoples of the planet Earth, I am establishing a worldwide *Fuck-*

A-Day Foundation, based on the indisputably valid theory that 'A Fuck a Day Keeps the Shrink Away . . .' ''

"How marvelous!" I gushed. "Why, you've even come up with your own opening slogan."

Her eyes were glazed by now, her gaze aimed at the distant heavens.

"Once daily at the least," she muttered, gripping the railing like a pulpit. "A sweet fuck each day for one and all, I pray."

I turned her over to Charles in her semi-trance, confident now that not even his silver tongue could penetrate her spiritual daze. She was truly happy now, not giddily so, as had been the case for the past week. Somehow I didn't mind losing her for the remainder of the cruise, especially to a cause rather than to Charles.

Countess Ulrica hurried over to me when she spotted me crossing the main cabin. "Did you hear that Valerie's leaving the ship later today?"

"I just found out."

"Aren't you going to talk her out of it?"

"Why? She's as happy as a nympho on a troopship. Her foundations are her life, Ulrica. They're actually orgasmic to her."

"The *Fuck-A-Day Foundation*?" she asked incredulously.

"It makes as much sense as most of them."

"Which means no sense," she sighed.

"Nonsense to us, perhaps, but very real and vital to her."

"Such a waste," Ulrica lamented. "She's so beautiful and kind and wealthy, and all she does is fritter her life away."

"Don't feel sorry for her, Countess. She's immeasurably happier than most people just doing her thing."

"I suppose," she conceded reluctantly. "How

about us going inside and doing our thing?''

I smiled. "I don't know about your thing, but my thing is hot as hell.''

"Have you had your fuck yet today?'' she inquired impishly.

"My foundation calls for ten a day, not one.''

"Enroll me,'' she laughed.

"I'll enroll you in the hay.''

Along the way, we enlisted a surprised but willing Dr. Henri Chartres in our boudoir expedition.

"You conducted a sleep experiment,'' I told him. "Now join us in a wide-awake test.''

"What does it entail?'' he inquired en route to Ulrica's quarters next to the captain's suite.

"It entails the tails of the three of us,'' I replied. "We want to see how many pieces we can knock off without destroying any of the wholes.''

"The whole holes?''

"A sort of theory of relativity. The formula is you-over-me-under-she.''

"Equals three pee over three,'' Dr. Henri joined in the silly parlay.

"That is if you're obeying the Golden Shower Rule,'' I noted.

"How can one take a piece from a hole when a hole is a vacuum?'' Ulrica questioned.

"All these perplexing queries and more will be investigated and hopefully resolved in our experiments in erotic evolution about to get under way in the laboratory of Countess Ulrica von Hoffman,'' I declared grandly as we arrived at her door.

The countess zeroed in on Dr. Henri's cock like a vulture on a snake the moment the door closed behind us. His prick swelled like a peacock showing its feathers as she sucked him savagely, both hands gripping its base. I pulled off her clothes after removing my own, then reached under her to grab at least a pound of pure cunt hanging between her shapely shanks. Ulrica had always had a superbly meaty crotch, the prime fuck meat a rosy pink and garnished with tawny curls. My tongue soon followed the route of my hand as I knelt behind her and inserted my face in the tempting crevice between her rounded cheeks.

"Men always make passes at girls with hot asses," Dr. Henri paraphrased a popular poet.

He reached for me, but could not make it without sacrificing deep-throating depth. His hands settled instead on Ulrica's lovely jiggling jugs with their nipples like scarlet thimbles.

"Let me come on them," he begged her as he played.

I buried myself even more deeply in the luscious labyrinth of her cunt as she leaned back to accommodate Henri's heavy hard-on between her mounds of milk.

"Suck her, Nicole," the professor encouraged me. "I'll fuck her tit while you lick her split."

I fingered myself as I sucked, strumming my clit like a harp. Whenever I was engrossed in choice cunnilingus such as now, I came repeatedly in a kind of orgasmic Morse code—long dashes of climax, followed alternately by brief, dramatic dots of orgasms. I knew it was the same with Ulrica; we had discussed it often and at length, masturbating during our dialogues to increase the enjoyment of the talks.

Dr. Henri was a groaner. So many men adhered to the strong, silent mold, it was refreshing to hear some audible expressions of enjoyment for a change. I glanced up and saw his cock was as red as a rooster's crest, swollen to the bursting point. Directly ahead of me there was a bright flush of color in Ulrica's cunt resembling a sunrise, a sure signal that she, too, was about to succumb to a massive orgasm.

He erupted first, splashing eggy come like a gourmet glaze over her heaving breasts. The warm ooze must have triggered her own major orgasm. Her thighs locked about my head, squeezing me in their fleshy vise. I had no choice but to share in the convulsions and contractions that coursed through her body. My anatomy was almost as attached to her for the time being as if we had been born Siamese twins, and the steady flow of mucilage from the mouth of her pussy ensured that the union was binding.

None of us was satisfied with just this single encounter as a trio. Dr. Henri insisted on eating us both, fucking us both anally and vaginally, and then sharing the champagne of his cock with us along with a blending of our own. Wet but happy, we rejoined the revelers on deck, passing Gilda performing expert fellatio on Count Erich in the cabin next to us. He waved casually to us, much as if he were merely having his shoes shined or his nails manicured.

"Gilda is down for the count," I noted punningly.

"He claims it lowers his blood pressure," Ulrica commented tolerantly.

"I would think it would raise it," Dr. Henri opined. "After all, the penis depends upon a rush of blood to its erectile tissues to achieve a hard-on."

"Whatever," the countess dismissed the subject airily. "As long as it keeps him healthy."

I was more surprised than the others to discover that Aunt Valerie had already disembarked and was en route to Paris. Had we been trysting that long?

"She left ahead of schedule," one of the ship's

officers explained. "A taxi driver made a deal with her from the river bank."

"It's not like her not to say good-bye," I said.

"She said you were following the credo of her new crusade," the officer reported. "Whatever that means."

"My fuck for the day," I muttered, smiling.

"Your what—?" he leaned forward to inquire.

"Oh, nothing," I replied. "It's just a private joke between us."

So Auntie was off and we were still on—for many more miles and many more days. I would miss her, of course, but not for long. The officer who had related the news of her departure had a virile handsomeness about him that was considerably enhanced by his deep-blue uniform.

"What is your name?" I inquired, skimming his physique with my eyes.

"Curt. Curt Weber."

"Did my Aunt Valerie tell you about her new cause?" I asked coyly.

"No, ma'am, she didn't."

"Are you interested?" I asked, flashing a tantalizing look in his direction.

"That depends." He smiled.

"Come to my cabin, and I'll tell you about it."

He glanced at his watch. "I'll be off duty in forty minutes. Will I still be in time for the lecture?"

"Definitely, and for the demonstration, too."

Aunt Val was soon forgotten, but another passionate disciple was recruited for her cause. The trip was going smoothly—very smoothly—and if it was do-or-die for Dumont, I was doing all I could to keep it lively.

chapter twenty-two

Passau. Linz. Krems. And then Vienna.

We sailed with leisurely abandon through the picturesque Austrian countryside, peering over the flats of abdomens and small rises of bellies, through the shrubbery of pubic hairs, relinquishing hardly a moment of intercourse, fellatio, or cunnilingus to view the riverside panorama unfolding before us.

Sighting down the barrel of a hardened cock or gazing through the sight formed by a pair of firm tits, we looked and licked, danced and dicked in lazy licentiousness for days on end, oblivious to the cares of the world so near and yet so far.

I ignored the calls from my lawyer Lamont Tyler in New York and contacted no one beyond shipboard, not even ever loyal and loving Peter Theophilus. Our ship was like a magic carpet adrift over the earth, within sight of everything yet in touch with nothing. It was a marvelous sojourn of *sans souci*, and I reveled in it totally.

However, there was a reality and terra firma on which it existed and we made a brief reacquaintance with it near Vienna. There, looming high above us one morning, was the formidable and familiar outline of Castle von Hoffman.

"A man's home is his castle," Count Erich declared from the bridge, "and my castle is my home. You are all invited to be my guests for a picnic and pig roast, after which we will continue our journey to Budapest and beyond."

The crowd cheered—a change of pace was always welcome even at an orgy—and in short order, the S.S. *Johann Sebastian* was deserted except for a skeleton crew. Even the captain accepted the invitation.

For me, as always, a return to the place I thought of as home was filled with nostalgic memories. Countess Ulrica knew this and consequently sought me out in the stampede down the gangplank.

"Come," she beckoned, "we'll ride until things calm down."

It seemed like an ideal escape plan, and I followed her willingly to a riverside shed where a pair of bicycles were stored. The stables were on the other side of the estate, a distance of a few miles.

"I haven't ridden a bike in ages," I laughed as the pointed seat mudged its way into the nook of my groin.

"It takes a bit more effort than riding a horse," she responded, "but it has its rewards—just like the stallions."

We passed over a bumpy stretch of earth as she spoke, sending erotic shock waves through my system. The rough terrain obviously had the same effect on her.

"Oooooh," she exclaimed, "that was delicious!"

I grinned in agreement. "These are definitely male cycles."

The Dumont crowd had gathered mostly on the broad terraces surrounding the castle. There food and drink abounded, along with strolling musicians and a troupe of near-naked dancers. Count Erich had always been a marvelous and generous host, sparing no expense to make his entertainments memorable. The sight of so many friends having fun removed any guilt I might have felt over ducking away so immediately after arrival. I vowed to return to them as soon as my ride with Ulrica was over.

"Such a lovely group of people," the countess commented as we skirted the populated patios in favor of the open meadow leading to the stables.

"That's why I'm pedaling my ass among them."

"Nicole!" she reacted in mock dismay.

"Just speaking my piece."

"You sound as if you're going to pieces."

"It'll all come together in one big piece," I assured her.

"This trip so far has been one piece after another," she noted. "Big and little."

"Have you had a chance at Tommy Riddle yet?"

"Who's he?"

"You haven't, then, or you'd remember. We girls nicknamed him 'Cannon'—and we weren't referring to his flatulence."

She glanced at me, her eyes sparkling. "He's endowed?"

"Like the main tower of an Ivy League college."

"Point him out to me later."

"I'll do more than that, I'll put him into you."

She smiled slyly. "You've always been such a

sweetly accommodating child."

Gunther had the stables as antiseptic as conditions allowed. It had always amazed me how neatly he maintained the buildings and stalls, considering the lack of cooperation from his equine charges.

"Greetings, Gunther," I called out from the doorway. "We've come back to haunt you and your horses."

"Welcome," he said, his customary opening bashfulness belied by the bold rise of his crotch. "I've had Rogue and Cocaine ready for you for hours."

"You knew we were coming?" Countess Ulrica asked, surprised.

"Count Erich radioed ahead," he told us. "I simply assumed you'd want to stretch your sea legs into saddles when you got here."

"Your assumption was astute," I said. "We both want to get away for a little while. The party's been going on for weeks."

"You look none the worse for wear," he commented.

"Our bodies are very resilient," the countess said.

"Particularly at the entrances," I said in titillation.

Gunther's jeans jumped at the groin.

"We'll be back shortly," Ulrica declared, flicking at the disturbance in his pants before mounting her pet stallion.

He doubled up momentarily, chuckling in surprise.

"You're handy and handsome," I teased. "So get handy with your hands some."

He simulated masturbation as we trotted off on our steeds.

"He's so spoiled," Ulrica complained. "He

thinks he should have some sort of sexual action every time anyone takes out one of his horses."

"That's horseshit," I commented. "I think we've both been more than generous with our genitals where he's concerned."

"I think it's being around stallions so much that makes him that way," she conjectured.

"Then let him fuck the mares," I declared airily.

"I wouldn't put that past him," she said nonchalantly.

"Remember the time he lost a bet with us and had to give an enema to Rogue?" I recalled, laughing at the recollection.

"He's still embarrassed about that," she reported.

"It was all in fun," I said. "Hell, you and I have done more drastic things than that."

"Shhh," she cautioned, finger to her lips.

"Why don't we bring some of the girls to the stables later?" I asked in a burst of inspiration. "I'll bet Cody and Simone—to name just two—would get a kick out of a little erotic equestrienne activity."

"Do you think so?" she asked with a shade of skepticism. "They might just get a kick, too. The horses aren't always in the mood for amateur saddle-humpers."

"It's just an idea," I retreated. "I'll hint around about it later and see what reaction I get."

"Erich had an idea last night," she revealed. "I don't know if he's still going to go through with it—but he wanted to get everyone in the party to go to the meadow for a mass moonlight fuck. How does that strike you?"

"Just the way it would strike you or a ewe," I punned. "Right in the valentine of the crotch."

"You like it, then?"

"Love it. Can't you just picture all these sheep-skin-oriented men like Dr. Beau, Roderick, René, Dr. Luke, Claude Reims and Dr. Henri submitting their credentials with all that genuine sheepskin wandering around? Baa! Humbuggery! It's a delicious setting. Let's work on Erich to make sure he goes through with it."

"He's ready, woolly, and able," she assured me. "I'm not so sure the sheep will like having their slumber disturbed by a bunch of fucking human animals."

"Don't worry about them," I laughed. "They'll love all the academic atmosphere."

"Nothing sheepish about you, Nicole. Maybe it'll inspire the animals to multiply."

"That's simple arithmetic, but I don't think they can add up to sixty-nine."

The countess smiled. "You're impossible, but adorable."

And thus it came to pass that the entire drunken mass of Dumont sheepskinners and their amorous allies gathered in the moonlit meadows of the von Hoffman estate to prove that where there's a wool, there's a lay. The bleating of lambs and the baaing of sheep accompanied the squeals and moans of alumnae, faculty, and friends alike being impaled on the pricks and tongues of professors and postgraduates in hungry harmony.

"I feel like Mary of the nursery rhyme," someone declared in the darkness. "I just had a little wham-bam, and my come was white as snow."

"Then I feel like Little Boy Blue," another announced, "because I found a creep in the meadow and he blew my horn."

The revelry continued well into the night, delaying our planned departure at dawn. But that was just as well, since exhaustion began to set in with daylight. A group of alumnae had utilized the cover of darkness to ambush Dr. Beauregard, strip him and tie him up and then cover his body with rock salt. Bozo was then deposited in the midst of all to serve as a human salt lick. We all watched covertly as he came time after time as the result of the enthusiastic lapping of his body, his cock and his balls by colleagues and coeds alike.

I fell asleep on the grass, only to be awakened by the prodding of Dr. Duncan's rigid rod.

"Roderick!" I gasped. "You're fucking me in broad daylight."

"Thou art a broad, so to speak, and my intention is to fucketh the daylights out of thee."

"How appropriate," I sighed. "Remember what Confucius say? Man who fuck woman on hill not on level."

"Be still! The moment doth not bode well for levity."

"Okay, prayers, then. Now I lay me down to fuck . . ."

"The moment cometh," he interrupted.

"I'm coming in a moment, too."

"Oh, how grand and glorious the fountain!" he cried out as his cock turned into a geyser, spewing lacy flakes of come over my belly and into the golden pelt of my pussy.

"Put it in again," I directed. "I'll keep it hard for you."

He redeposited his cock in my cave and I promptly clutched its head with my vaginal muscles. The action spread its effect through my body, culminating in a classic come that bordered on a convulsion. I shook with passion as his prick resumed its pounding, driving a stake into the heart of my haunches.

No one paid particular attention to our intense intercourse. Those who were not engaged in doing the same with someone else were slumbering peacefully in the morning sun.

Count Erich had one of his servants sound reveille on a long trumpet, a signal to summon all of us back to the ship. The day and night of land-lubbering licentiousness was ending. It was back to the Danube for the disciples of Dumont—there to resume our river revelry across the remainder of Austria and on into Czechoslovakia and Hungary.

chapter twenty-three

Somehow I had not encountered Gilda for days despite our proximity aboard ship and at the castle. I could only attribute that to the probability that she was so busy pointing her legs to the stars in secluded hideaways that our paths simply had not crossed. When I did see her finally while sunning on the after deck, my speculation was confirmed in a hilarious way—or so I thought initially. There came Gilda wearing a full-fledged muzzle of the type used on dangerous dogs.

"What in hell—?" I began questioning her, only to be interrupted by her voluntary explanation.

"René made me put it on," she said with a none-too-convincing laugh. "He said I've been sucking too much cock and cunt."

"So he muzzled you?" I inquired incredulously. "What are we—back in the Dark Ages?"

"He won't have anything more to do with me until I wear it for one full day."

"Twenty-four hours?"

"Two dozen successive segments of sixty minutes each," she confirmed.

"The man's a maniac!"

"That's what he calls me, a sex maniac."

"That's the only acceptable species."

"He's not really joking, Nicole. He says I'm suffering from an acute case of chronic nymphomania."

"What a delightful disease," I kidded her. "What brought all this on anyhow?"

"Just what I said. He followed me around for two days chronicling all my cock and cunt capers."

"He's not your chaperone," I reminded her. "He's got no right."

"No, but he knows I dig him."

"You should bury him for this. A joke is a joke, but the more I think about it, the more outrageous this is."

"I've already completed eleven hours. I just couldn't stay inside my cabin any longer."

"That bastard! Bite his cock the next time he wants you to suck it."

"Maybe I need the punishment. René thinks I'm entirely too undisciplined."

"Let him work on Bozo. At least there his efforts would be appreciated."

"I think he *does* spank Dr. Beau now and then."

"But you're not into that obedience shit, are you?" I asked her. "I never noticed any sign of it with you."

Gilda shrugged. "Who knows? All I can say is I don't really—I mean really, really—mind wearing this for him. If it gives him satisfaction, what the hell? Twenty-four hours out of a lifetime isn't much."

"No, maybe not, but more than likely, he'll have you in and out of that thing like a kennel owner taming a bad bitch."

Gilda smiled wanly. "As long as he fucks me," she sighed.

I left her in her facial harness, mildly disgusted by her uncharacteristic submissiveness. There was nothing so special about René Tremain to warrant her ready capitulation to his cockeyed commands.

"Look me up when you get out of the mask," I told her. "You're much too attractive to hide behind a grate."

By chance I encountered Tommy Riddle moments later. We were both going in the same direction—to the forward part of the ship.

"Did you see Gilda in that doggie getup?" he asked me immediately.

"Woof!"

"Is she stoned, or what the fuck's wrong with her?"

"She's suffering from academic aftermath," I diagnosed. "All through school she fantasized fucking Monsieur Tremain—and now she's his love slave."

"I can't believe that about Gil. She'd tell the pope to go take a flying fuck."

"That's what I always thought—until now."

"Next thing'll be a muzzle on her muff," he predicted. "Then her legs'll atrophy from lack of spreading."

"You have a vivid imagination."

"And you have a vivid vagina."

"Speaking of the latter, how about giving a demonstration of the tensile strength of your tool for the countess?"

"Ulrica? From what I've seen of her, I'd fuck her anytime."

"How about right now?"

"Is this a setup or something?" he asked warily.

"Make it lucky coincidence on your part. She's the local royalty, so I thought it would be nice if you fired a salute from your cannon."

He grinned, proud as always of any recognition accorded his oversized organ.

"It's loaded for bare. Bare ass."

The countess was supervising preparations for an evening buffet in the main cabin, but she quickly disposed of her duties upon introduction to Tommy.

"Nicole tells me you were something of a campus visitors' phenomenon," she gushed as we three scurried to her stateroom.

"He was the unofficial campus prick," I couldn't resist commenting.

"I held my own," Tommy doubled an entendre.

"We used to pet it like an animal," I recalled. "He always aired it between his legs during visits."

"And between asses after classes," he parlayed a play on words. "I slipped into dorms during those last few months."

"I'll bet you were in much demand," Ulrica flattered him.

"Let's say that I jerked off only for the novelty of it, never due to necessity."

"Cocky, isn't he?" I noted.

"Just aware," he disagreed. "But in a physiological sense, I might agree with you."

"Cocky both ways," I retorted.

Countess Ulrica cared little for our conversation, pro or con, being enthralled only with the prospect of sampling his super schwantz. Her eyes were beady with eagerness as I made a dramatic, opening curtain pull of his fly, the head emerging like that of a stallion from its stall.

"Ohhhh!" she gasped as it forged forward, supported by a shaft like the long neck of a swan. "How spectacular!"

As I had promised, I seized it behind the head in the manner of subduing a poisonous snake and then fed the throbbing crown toward Ulrica's seething pussy. She had fallen back and grabbed her ankles in an effort to provide the maximum measure of meat for the hungry monster.

"Ready! Aim! Fuck!" I shouted as Tommy's tool forded her fuck flesh.

"Godddddamnnnnnn!" she shrieked at the invasion of her pubes.

"A royal fuck, remember?" I reminded Tommy, slapping him on his bare buttocks.

"She's got a pussy as plump as my prick," he noted in quick gasps.

"Give her a drenching," I said. "Flood her with come."

"Just fuck me," the countess pleaded, her brow furrowed from the sweet agony of absorbing such thickness and pounding. "The come will come naturally."

He bored into her with gusto, sinking his shaft like a wildcatter drilling for oil. It was a voyeur's delight watching their heated quest for climax. To add inspiration to the attainment, I knifed my tongue into the crack of Tommy's ass, causing his cheeks to twitch and tighten as he drove even deeper into Ulrica's capacious cunt.

"Oooooh," he whistled, "you *do* do the sweetest things, baby!"

It was only a matter of time before the grunting and groaning turned urgent. I knew from experience that Ulrica was in the throes of orgasm for several minutes before a rich load of come tumbled from the tip of Tommy's tool. The countess reveled in the residue, finger-painting her abdomen with the slippery silver of his sperm.

"I'd like to stable you at the castle," she told him when he finally withdrew from her well. "You're absolutely divine, young man."

"Not really," he responded with surprising modesty, "it's just the music of my organ that makes you think that."

"It's heavenly," she confirmed.

"Did I deliver?" I asked her, seeking a bit of credit for my part in the performance.

"You delivered," she agreed, "and he *really* delivered."

"If Gilda has to wear a muzzle," I said to Tommy, "maybe you need a harness."

"He's too gentle for that," he replied, petting his prick. "He never bites—just spits at pretty pussies."

"Dr. Duncan would call it sexpectorating," I noted.

"You should know," he retorted. "I saw him dunkin' in your donut the other night."

"You weren't supposed to be watching," I chided him.

"If you can be a voyeur, so can I."

"Which is my clue to get back on deck and into action," I responded.

"I'll seize you later," Tommy jibed.

"One if by land, two if by sea."

"The cannon will roar," he promised.

"Ulrica," I called to her from the passageway, "I'll see you at the buffet."

"Yes, darling," she replied.

Out on the main deck I found a still-muzzled Gilda being entertained by Charles Leroux.

"Watch him," I warned her, "he's armed with a pen and dangerous."

"Will you get off my case, please, Nicole?" he reacted with a look of chagrin. "I *do* talk to lovely people for reasons other than gathering book information."

"Muzzled misses?"

He turned to look at Gilda again. "Isn't it delightfully idiotic?" he asked, obviously intrigued by the situation.

"I'm sure that the sequel to *The Adultery Commitment* will include a sensual lady similarly restrained," I predicted.

"It's original," he commented.

"Not with you, however," I reminded him.

"I am an observer as well as an inventor of characters and situations," he defended himself.

"The least you could do is to offer the orally limited lady a little erotic entertainment to ease her burden," I suggested.

"A tongue-lashing perhaps?" he proposed with a glint in his eyes.

"You wouldn't mind being muffed with a mask on, would you, honey?" I questioned Gilda.

"You make it sound so staged," she objected. "Charles is perfectly capable of articulating his own propositions."

"Pardon me," I said with feigned annoyance, turning on my heels.

"Just kidding," she called after me.

I kept on walking, my mood unsettled for some reason or another. Perhaps it was the weeks of cavorting with the same crowd that was beginning to get to me. I knew myself well enough to know that I could not endure cruising the Danube for too much longer. Nicole was meant to float on the zephyrs and dance through the stars, never to tarry long in any one place or with any one group or individual.

"Thy head is in the clouds, I do perceive," the familiar voice of Rod Duncan interrupted my musing.

"Hello, Rod," I replied rather flatly.

"Depression in the midst of elation? The immortal Bacchus, god of wine and revelry, wouldst smite thee for despairing under bacchanalian conditions akin to these."

I forced a thin smile. "I probably need to be muzzled like Gilda, and corked as well."

"Wouldst thou permit me the honor and privilege of banging in the bung?" he kidded me.

"The hole is not holy, so the rite is wholly thine," I responded in kind.

The merest suggestion of sex between us invariably caused Dr. Duncan's shorts to wiggle. Somehow just being with him lifted my spirits in much the same manner that our togetherness lifted his cock.

"My cabin awaits," he said with a sweeping gesture.

I followed his lead almost mechanically. My spring was wound tightly, so directions proved easy to follow. I really did not feel like thinking, and having someone I trusted to direct me at this time was unexpectedly salutary.

"You're so learned, Roderick," I told him once we were inside his cabin. "I'm surprised you're also so lustful."

"The aesthetics of the Greeks appeal to me," he said, dropping his fancy language momentarily, "but the cruder carnality of the Romans really bubbles my blood."

"They were sexually more savage and sadistic, weren't they?" I recalled from ancient history classes.

"Thou art correct," he reverted to his usual jargon. "They produced no thinkers like Thales and Heraclitus, no artist like Phidias, nor poets like Alcaeus and Sappho. All theoretical activities such as art, science, and philosophy were beyond the Roman grasp."

"You're not beyond my grasp, however," I

said, clutching a fistful of his emerging cock.

"Thou showest the cruel grasp of Nero in thy hand."

"But my lips will be soft as Sappho."

"So be it, fair maiden," he said as I knelt to receive his scepter.

The head slid into my mouth with smooth certainty. I then fingered his organ like a musical instrument, my tongue the reed that fluctuated to perform a rhapsody.

"I quote from the great lyric poet Horace," he declared in an emotion-filled voice, "that you might be inspired by his words in thy labor of love . . ."

. . . And when your lust is hot, surely
if a maid or pageboy's handy, to attack
instanter, you won't choose to grin and bear
    it?
I won't! I like a cheap and easy love!

My lips withdrew from his cock head so rapidly that the resulting suction sound echoed through the cabin.

"A cheap and easy love is it?" I shrieked. "Why, you fucking sonofabitch!"

"Oh, no!" he cried out. "Thou misunderstandeth, darling Nicole, love! 'Twas Horace I quote, not Roderick Duncan."

"I'm on my knees sucking your prick, dear Dr. D," I fumed, "and you choose from your literary grab bag a quotation from Roman history that refers to cheap and easy love. With your intelligence, that has to be more than coincidental."

"I beg of you not to misinterpret my intent," he pleaded. "Would that I could retrieve my words and choose from Lord Byron or Keats or Wordsworth instead. But Horace inflames my libido with his lusty insinuations, and thus I selfishly chose a passage to compliment the exotic pleasures of your mouth upon me."

I stood before him, watching his cock slowly collapse. "That's a pretty fancy defense, professor," I told him. "Maybe I did jump the gun a bit in making my inferences."

"You were always an 'A' student of mine," he responded. "Your clearheaded logic remains intact."

"I'll get back to giving clear head if you refrain from any more quotes," I bargained.

"Thou art eminently fair, my fair maiden," he replied. "Kindly proceed with thine most felicitous fellatio."

"I bow to the unsheathed sword before me," I proclaimed, "succumbing once more as thy supplicant."

"Suck come, my supplicant."

Spared the indignity of being a cheap and easy love, I nonetheless managed a cheap and easy come. The brief dispute charged us both with extra passion, enabling me to achieve a climax in close conjunction to his. Come circled like a smoke ring around the head of his cock as I waved it about my face, savoring the shower of gelatinous sperm spurting from the tip.

Dr. Duncan insisted thereafter on reading dozens of love poems and sonnets to me to assure me of his deep and abiding affection as well as his remorse over the quote from Horace. Later, with the love lyrics drifting about my mind, we made a silent vow of lasting friendship in the sweetest of all ways—a sustained, evening-long session of sixty-nining that lasted clear to the border of Czechoslovakia.

chapter twenty-four

It had been the *Donau* in Germany and it became the *Dunaj* as we entered Czechoslavakia at Bratislava. Across the border in Hungary it would soon become the *Duna*. But it was still the Danube, and we were still the girls and guests of Dumont sailing along it.

But some attrition had begun to set in. The departures had begun with Aunt Valerie, and ever since, singles and pairs had defected for various personal and business reasons. Not everyone—not even every Académie Dumont graduate—had the luxury of unlimited free time enjoyed by the likes of Gilda and myself.

The first really noticeable group departure, however, occurred just before we reached the Czech border near Petrzalka. The prospect of entering a Soviet satellite country was anathema to a surprising number of alumnae. It took a chartered bus to cart off the large contingent of faculty and former classmates who chose to abandon the S.S.

Johann Sebastian at that point of the journey. Among them was Dr. Marcel Beauregard, Monsieur René Tremain (good news for Gilda, I rejoiced), and, to my sorrow, Dr. Roderick Duncan.

"It's so silly," I protested at our parting.

"It's a matter of principle."

"You put principle ahead of pleasure?"

"Reluctantly, but with conviction."

"I suppose I should admire you," I retorted, "but I think you're just being pigheaded."

"As a man soweth, so shall he rape," he replied with a tolerant smile.

"I got the swinish pun. Don't think it eluded me."

"Thou art a true darling," he whispered in our final embrace. "Be not a stranger at thine alma mater."

There was a strange aura of emptiness after the bus had departed and the ship resumed its slow, steady run southward. Nobody talked much as we hung from the upper-deck railings trying to discern precisely where and when we would be leaving the free world to enter Communist-controlled territory. Of course there was no line of distinction anywhere in the rolling farmland before us. Cattle grazed and grain grew with idyllic indifference to the politics of the mortals among them. I myself was an internationalist, if anything, a free spirit who recognized no boundaries and no ideologies save sybaritic abandon. Make love, not war was as close to being my motto as anything I had ever read and remembered from the walls of Aunt Valerie's offices.

"May I join you in your meditations?" First Officer Curt Weber inquired.

"It's your ship."

"Hardly, but I don't want to annoy you if

you'd prefer to be alone."

"I almost never *prefer* to be alone. It's just that I may not be very good company right at the moment."

"You are good company just being next to someone," he said with sincerity.

"Thank you. Maybe you can tell me when we go from fairyland to the land of the big, bad wolf."

"I thought Russia was symbolized by a bear."

"You must bear with my ignorance," I responded lightly.

"I think you'll find Budapest is still enchanting. We're not just going from sunlight to eternal darkness, or anything like that."

"I didn't think so. I've done my share of peeking behind the Iron Curtain."

"I'm sure of that," he agreed.

"Those flashing lights up ahead"—I pointed— "what do they mean?"

Curt chuckled. "They mean we're about to be boarded by the big, bad border inspectors for the big, bad bear."

"Like customs?"

"Only more so."

"Meaner?"

He hesitated. "More coolly efficient, I'd say," he elaborated. "More militaristic, as you'd expect in a police state."

"I hope they're not opposed to sexual intercourse as they are to intercourse among nations," I ventured.

He smiled briefly. "They're still human, though you might get some arguments on that point at times."

"Will we be searched?" I asked with slight apprehension.

"The ship will be. Individual inspection will

depend on the commandant."

"This may be sort of exciting."

Curt smiled mischievously. "You like the idea of being stripped?"

"It depends. Both Gilda and I are exhibitionists at heart."

"And rightly so. You have endowments well worth exhibiting."

"You're cute. Remind me to recommend you for promotion."

"My next step up is to captain. How about making me master of your fate?"

"And captain of my hole?"

"A classic idea."

"I'll issue you a poetic license," I joked.

"I wouldn't suggest being so witty with our invading force," he advised. "I've yet to meet one border guard with even a shred of humor."

"Maybe I should get down to just a shred of clothing," I suggested. "Every little tit helps."

Curt surveyed me good-naturedly. "You're hardly overdressed as is, nor are your breasts little by any scale of measurement."

"A merchant mariner with a silver tongue," I declared. "What a unique combination."

"No more so than a golden goddess with a sterling sense of humor."

"Careful," I cautioned. "You could be arrested for being a salt and flattery."

"Ugh!" he groaned. "That's hitting below decks."

Our cheerful prattle ended abruptly with the barking of a voice over a bullhorn.

"Attention you aboard the S.S. *Johann Sebastian!*" it rasped. "Prepare for immediate boarding by officers of the Committee for International Border Control! Ship clearances and individual passport documentation are required to be available for immediate examination before permission can be granted to proceed!''

"We are standing by as directed," our captain announced from the bridge. "Crew is starboard to assist members of your party in boarding."

"Aren't you needed there?" I asked Curt.

"I'm off duty," he replied. "Besides, I might push them backward instead of helping them aboard."

"You wouldn't!"

He laughed lightly. "Probably not. I don't relish being imprisoned on this side of the border."

"You don't normally sail this far on the river, do you?"

"No. Our regular run ends at Vienna, well within the free world, thank God."

"There won't be any problem, of course. Will there? I'd expect that Count Erich made sure all the arrangements were set for a smooth sailing."

"The Communists always give you some hassle," he replied. "There's no such thing as carte blanche east of the Austrian border."

"They're probably just jealous of our luxurious life-style."

"Jealous or not, we're in their jurisdiction, so it pays to cooperate."

"Not if it means sacrificing any of the fun so far," I pouted.

Curt patted my hand reassuringly. "The fun will return," he promised. "Just put yourself on 'hold' for a few minutes."

A squad of six men, armed and wearing dull-green uniforms with red and black epaulets, clambered noisily over the railing of the ship and gathered in a loose knot on deck. Our captain was there to greet them, hardly with much enthusiasm, while Count Erich stood by his side. The senior member of the entourage stepped forward,

196

flashlight in hand, to examine the papers handed him by the captain.

"You are without specific destination?" he looked up to interrogate the captain.

"We sail to Budapest, and certification has been obtained to continue on, possibly to Yugoslavia and Rumania."

The border official eyed him suspiciously. "A ship of this size and capacity with no definite destination, captain? Isn't that rather unusual?"

"We are on a charter cruise," the captain explained patiently. "Count Erich here has hired the *Johann Sebastian* for a pleasure voyage for himself and his guests with no fixed termination date or location."

"Capitalistic excess," he hissed at the count. "All right, let's proceed with the individual scrutiny. Carl, Boris, work aft to midship. Walter, John come with me to the forward section."

They paired off quickly and proceeded briskly to their assigned areas.

"I'd like to borrow Gilda's muzzle and put it on him," I whispered to Curt. "He looks like a bulldog."

"Careful," Curt cautioned. "Remember what I told you about flippancy with these birds."

"Vultures!" I whispered.

He shook his head in mild exasperation. Keeping me quiet could be a problem at times, especially if I was being pushed around. So far, however, they had been all bluster, and I could cope with that if not quite accept it.

"You!" the head of the group called out from the bridge, pointing at me. "Come here, please!"

"Not him, too?" I retorted, indicating Curt.

"You!" he repeated. "Alone!"

"Good luck," Curt whispered.

"My papers are in order," I told him.

"I hope the same applies to their manners," he said.

I felt the slightest tinge of anxiety after that remark. It was the first time since sighting the patrol boat that I had even the smallest measure of concern over what I had considered a routine official nuisance.

I was surprised to find Gilda in the pilot house when I arrived there. She looked apprehensive, at first, but relaxed somewhat upon sighting me.

"Gil," I greeted her, "fancy meeting you here."

"Unmuzzled and uncertain," she replied.

The head policeman, whose rank I couldn't determine from his sleeve markings, was busying himself with a sheaf of documents spread over the navigational maps. He pretended not to be listening or paying any attention to us, but I was an excellent student of male slyness and craftiness in observing females covertly. We were alone with him in the semicircular room with its sweeping glass windows, a situation I found a bit unlikely and unnerving.

"Ladies," he turned to address us finally, "I am Lieutenant Jan Kollar of the Czech border police. I trust you have your passports and visas for me to examine."

"Yes," I answered immediately, extending mine.

"Right here," Gilda replied, also holding out hers.

He took the booklets and attendant papers in his hand, but instead of looking at them he stared at us instead.

"I would much prefer to examine both of you," he confessed with a lascivious leer. "Your papers are in no way comparable to the bodies they represent."

Gilda and I exchanged uneasy glances.

"What do you mean by that, Lieutenant?" I managed to ask.

"In many years of service to my government, never have I encountered two such beautiful young women traveling together. One, occasionally, but then always in the company of a drab. Never a pair of ravishing ladies such as you."

"You're very kind," Gilda said with a gulp.

Her obvious nervousness made me nervous. Lt. Kollar was anything but a handsome man, more closely resembling a uniformed toad. Not only was he fat and warty, but he breathed heavily through his nostrils, and little clusters of saliva bubbled at the corners of his mouth.

"I've made a discretionary decision regarding both of you," he announced, removing his bandolier and the holstered gun attached to it. "Rather than review your documentation, I will determine your admissibility into Czechoslovakia on the basis of your physical credentials. Are you in agreement with that procedure?"

Kollar's cock was at full mast inside his uniform as he studied us with a lecherous grin.

I swallowed hard and looked at Gilda. Her eyes mirrored her fright. It was up to me to make the decision—and there was really only one choice to make.

"You want us naked?" I asked as evenly as I could.

He shrugged and his belly shook with a forced laugh. "How else does one examine a body?"

I started to strip when he interrupted.

"It would be better if one undressed the other," he instructed. "That is the procedural way the police prepare prisoners for examination."

Prisoners? The very word chilled my blood.

Even the sight of Gilda's gorgeous tits did nothing to warm it. Nor did the unveiling of her ripe sable cunt.

"Excellent," Kollar commented, a pool of saliva in his mouth making him gurgle as he spoke.

I got back some of my poise and confidence once my own pussy was exposed. It was like my badge of authority, my means of *cunt*rolling a situation.

The lieutenant was drooling openly by now. I taunted him by spreading the lips of my labia, creating a lovely rose blossom of raw fuck flesh.

"Come, Jan," I urged him, risking familiarity on the basis of my crotch appeal. "Suck it for me."

He hesitated only a moment, accepting his demotion to the deck as the price of my pussy. Gilda took a cue from me and pulled down his pants as he licked. She then applied her own mouth to his swollen prick, as thick and strong as the arm and fist in the Communist logo. For the time being, we were in total control of him. I could have grabbed his gun from the table, but what use would it serve? A suck and perhaps a fuck from now, we would be free to continue our trip down the Danube. It was something to endure, knowing it would soon end.

"Gobble him, Gilda," I encouraged her. "Blow his nuts!"

Kollar came like a cannon, spurting balls of pasty come all over Gilda and himself. Try as I did, I could not bring myself to climax. That made it a historic moment for me—as far as I could remember, I'd never failed under any conditions to come at least once from being sucked. The lieutenant rolled about on the deck after his massive orgasm, his eyes disorganized, his lips emitting low moans. It took him several minutes to regain his composure, if not his command presence. As I'd expected, he wanted to fuck us both, and we of course accommodated him.

"I should hold you here as hostages," he commented after his third come. "Your vulvas are too valuable to be allowed out of the country."

"We come from another *cunt*ry," I punned, forgetting Curt's earlier advice.

"You come here, too, no?"

"Magnificently," I lied.

He laughed again in his lewd manner. "Never have I had better. You deserve to be Czechs."

"That's a real compliment," I lied again, "but we're here to enjoy your country as visitors. From what I've seen so far, it's a lovely land."

"The best," he confirmed. "The Soviets are lucky to have us."

"Our papers are all in order, then?" Gilda asked.

"In perfect shape," he replied, handing them back to us.

"We're free to go, then?" Gilda asked with anxiety apparent.

"Just one more thing," Kollar said, reaching for his gun belt. "I have a little game I like to play with beautiful ladies."

"I thought we played all the games you like," I injected.

"Ho, ho," he chortled, "those are good games and you played them very well—but this is different."

Gilda and I flashed wary glances at one another. The feeling of uneasiness was returning despite the intimacy we'd developed with Kollar in such a brief time.

"I see down on deck that your men have finished all their work," I told him. "They keep looking up this way, apparently for you."

"Let them wait," he said sternly. "I am in charge here."

He took the gun out of its holster and began removing bullets from the chamber. My gaze was frozen on his hands as they moved with expertise about the blue steel barrel.

"Have you heard of roulette?" he asked, looking up at us.

"Yes," I admitted. "I play it at Monte Carlo all the time."

"Russian roulette?"

I gulped. "No," I said, just barely above a whisper.

"It is appropriate here in a Soviet satellite state, don't you think?" he asked, leering again.

"It's not real gambling," Gilda commented, her voice wavering.

"Oh, no?" He feigned amusement. "A single bullet in the gun, a flip of fate, and the barrel up your vagina? That is not a gamble?"

"I don't want to play that," I said firmly.

"Nor I," Gilda seconded.

His eyes narrowed and the saliva returned to the sides of his mouth. "You play it here and continue your cruise, or you play it at patrol headquarters maybe several dozen times and be sent back to Austria. It is very popular with the officers of the border patrol, particularly with such lovely young ladies."

"That doesn't leave us much choice," I said.

"Precisely," he agreed. "Now who wants to be first."

"I'll go first," I replied. "I don't *want* to go first."

"A beautiful pussy like yours could never be destroyed," he said confidently.

"Good luck," Gilda said softly as he stuck the

barrel of his pistol into my cunt.

"First we have a little extra fun. I like to jerk young ladies off with my trusty gun before pulling the trigger."

Perspiration appeared like dew all over my body as he slid the barrel deftly in and out of my pussy. Gilda stood with her eyes squeezed tightly shut, unable to bear witness.

"How does it feel?" the lieutenant asked, playing with one of my tits with his free hand while the other manipulated the gun.

"This is not my idea of a first-class romantic situation."

"The excitement should be erotic. Your body is as feverish as if you were in a passionate relationship."

"I like my guns attached to a scrotum, and firing only soft white bullets."

"Try to come," he urged. "It would please me greatly."

I faked a frantic orgasm just to get on with the tense situation. It seemed to fool Kollar, who stopped to watch my facial contortions and the quivering of my body.

"Good. Now comes the real climax. Are you ready?"

"As ready as I'll ever be," I replied in a strained voice.

"One, two, three," he counted. Then the trigger clicked.

I came truly, then, a tremendous rush of relief that swelled into a full, blessed orgasm.

"Now, wasn't that fun?" Kollar asked.

"It's a helluva way to come," I declared.

"Now it's Gilda's turn," he said, patting her prominent buttocks. "Bring that pretty pussy right squat down on this skinny prick of a pistol, and let's see how it goes with you."

Gilda's knees were trembling visibly as she lowered her sable snatch onto the end of the gun. The barrel disappeared into the whorl of flesh there with Kollar delightedly sliding it back and forth in the lush labyrinth.

"I want you to have just as good a come as Nicole," he told her. "Don't hold anything back."

"Nicole!" she cried. "I'm scared!"

"I'll pray for you," I assured her, recalling one of Dr. Luke's erotic entreaties.

"Fuck the gun, honey," the lieutenant encouraged her with a rare touch of sentiment. "You get off before he gets off."

Tense moments passed with Gilda actually humping the barrel as she would a cock.

Kollar was enchanted. "You could go in the Olympics with cunt control like that."

She eventually did come—actually and not acting, as I had done—and then came the countdown once again. Her eyes closed again as he counted slowly.

"One . . . two . . . three . . . " he enunciated.

Then—click!

I actually cheered as she fell back, safe and sound, the only wound in her womb the lovely laceration that was her natural cunt. She had come, too, I learned later—just as I had in a burst of grateful, glorious relief.

Lieutenant Kollar did not wait for us to dress before returning to his men on deck. There he was all business once more, stern and unyielding. We got there just as he was descending the rope ladder to the patrol boat.

"You!" he said demandingly, indicating me as he had earlier from the bridge. "Come here!"

With heart in mouth, I hurried to the rail fearful of a last minute complication. "What is it,

Lieutenant?" I asked anxiously.

"I just wanted you to know," he whispered confidentially, "there never was a bullet in my gun."

I burst into tears as the patrol boat roared off into the night. It was all too much. When I told Gilda moments later, we both dissolved in tears. Fun was fun, but even we had limits. When the Danube became the "Damn you," it was time to think about ending this seemingly endless escapade.

chapter twenty-five

Budapest was rather anticlimactic, but gastronomically delightful. Our thinning ranks of revelers were eager once again to abandon ship for land adventuring, assured that the Hungarian police were not gun-muzzle masturbators as our Czech cop had been. In fact, the city hardly seemed to have a military presence at all, resembling instead a lively West European metropolis.

Tommy Riddle felt comfortable enough to organize what he called a "pussy posse"—half a dozen male voyagers volunteering to join him on a "cunt hunt." They were determined to ravage a share of the local beauties, and failing that, resigned to resorting to prostitutes if necessary.

"Just to get something fresh to fuck," he explained to the jeers of all the girls aboard ship.

I was tempted to join the group myself, as was Gilda, but our tentative moves in that direction met with immediate rebuffs. It was to be a macho enterprise, we were told—no females allowed.

"Go fuck yourselves, then," Gilda retorted in no uncertain terms.

In that spirit of friendly dissension, we split into several different groups for our invasion of "the Paris of Eastern Europe." Gilda and I elected to join the count and countess, among others, since they were quite knowledgeable about the restaurants and nightlife of the city.

"Hungary can't be compared to any of the other Communist bloc countries," Count Erich informed us. "The food here in Budapest is unbelievably good—and plentiful."

"It'll be nice to sink my teeth into something besides cock and cunt for a change," Gilda whispered to me.

"I still wouldn't mind going with Tommy and his crew," I confessed. "The women here are exceptionally attractive."

"I detect a hunger for Hungarians in you," she said. "Maybe you could order one for dessert."

"How about an assortment? They come in different flavors."

"And you come in all of them," she jested.

I poked her playfully in the ribs. "Look who's talking! The girl most likely to suck seeds from anybody."

"Caraway seeds are big in Hungarian cuisine," Countess Ulrica commented, catching just a drift of our muted conversation.

"Good," I joked. "Gilda can get carried away sucking caraway seeds."

Count Erich loved to act as guide on any outing, and here in Budapest he was in his glory. The rest of us were too young to have his considerable knowledge of cities beyond the Iron Curtain. That afforded him the opportunity to be our instructor, a role he relished enough to have volunteered to be a guest lecturer at the Académie Dumont in the past.

"The state runs most of the restaurants these days," he informed us, "but in Budapest they've maintained surprising quality levels in food and service. I doubt whether it's what it was in the days of the Hapsburgs, but it's very good indeed."

"They put paprika on practically everything," Ulrica observed. "Theirs is so brilliantly red that it makes other versions pale by comparison."

"I'll put paprika on your pussy," I whispered to Gilda.

"A condiment for the cunt?"

"Pay attention to Erich," Ulrica chided us like schoolgirls caught gossiping in class.

"I'll tell you something about paprika," the count resumed his impromptu lecture. "What is known in most of the world as the bell pepper comes in Hungary in ivory, yellow, green, and red, depending on the season. The best comes from south-central Hungary, especially the towns of Kalocsa and Szeged . . . "

"Piss on all this paprika prattle," I muttered, setting Gilda giggling.

The count looked at her, vaguely annoyed. He seldom was serious, but when he was, he liked to be taken that way.

"Do you find paprika amusing, Gilda?" he inquired.

"Only the name." She stifled her titter.

"That is from the Magyar language," he explained. "The history of its introduction to Hungarian cuisine dates back to the Turkish conquest in 1526. The Turks ruled most of Hungary for 150 years and raised in their gardens the peppers they'd imported from India via Persia. When they finally left, the paprika stayed."

"Burp!" I teased Gilda, reviving her giggles.

What a silly mood we were in—from smoking pot all day—just when the count was so solemnly pedantic.

"Enough of this nostalgic nonsense," he declared with resignation. "Let's eat my words."

We followed him like the Pied Piper as he led us to a lovely old building where the Alabardos Restaurant was located. There Erich took charge of the ordering, pointing out that our food was being served on Herend porcelain.

"I always like to eat on her end," I quipped. "Especially Gilda's."

This time the count laughed jovially, his mood uplifted by the savory fragrances wafting through the dining room.

"You are irrepressible, dear Nicole. It's been such a joy to have you on the whole voyage."

"This is the finale, isn't it?" I asked. "I mean Budapest was to be our final destination, wasn't it?"

"That had been the tentative plan," he replied, glancing about at the others at the table. "However, there have been a number of requests to continue farther on the Danube, possibly to the Yugoslavian-Rumanian border. What would be your reaction to that, darling?"

I paused, hesitant to express my immediate thoughts on the unexpected proposition.

"I'd have to think about that," I hedged.

"You are having a good time, aren't you?"

"But of course, Count Erich. It's been the voyage of a lifetime, to date."

"Perhaps that's why we're all so reluctant to have it end," he surmised.

"I could go on and on," Countess Ulrica declared, "but the castle could disintegrate if we neglect it much longer."

"Bull dung!" the count exclaimed. "We have a staff that probably runs the place more efficiently without our interference, Ulrica. That is simply not a valid reason for cutting the cruise short."

"But, Erich," she protested, "we would not be cutting the cruise short—as Nicole has pointed out. We are in Budapest. And the original itinerary called for Black Forest-to-Budapest if you remember."

The count clearly did not want to remember. The trip had been a true tonic to him and it was obvious he did not want it to conclude—at least not yet.

"We will take a vote aboard ship later," he announced. "I will abide by the verdict of the majority."

"Shhhh," I kidded in an effort to avoid further conflict, "that's not a popular concept in a Communist country."

Count Erich smiled and nodded, toasting my comment with yet another glass of Pinot Noir from Villanyi, Hungary's southernmost city. We were all indulging heavily in a variety of local wines from Egri Bikaver to Keknyelu, mixing reds and whites indiscriminately like careless pseudo-connoisseurs.

"To Dumont," I proposed still another toast.

Glasses were raised and contents disappeared down already well-lubricated throats.

"To Count Erich," another suggested.

Empty glasses again.

"To the pussy posse," Gilda called out. "To the cunt hunt!"

It was a good thing the food began arriving about now. Otherwise all senses of taste would have been drowned in a sea of vintage wines.

Count Erich rose over the steaming dishes to insist on one final preprandial libation. "We must all have an aperitif dear to Hungarians," he announced. "Waiters, kindly pour barack for everyone."

The sweet apricot brandy tasted surprisingly good in spite of all the wine preceding it. It managed to reawaken appetites rather dulled by the wines. There was no interruption in the flow of wines throughout the meal either, but at least everyone was also busy indulging in the delicious entrées.

Frogs legs and snails, boar and venison, were among the items served us at our banquet-sized table. And of course there was the traditional *gulyas*—goulash to most of us—with tiny bits of pasta called *csipetke* and lots and lots of—what else?—paprika. Stuffed cabbage, too, and jokai bean soup with smoked ham and *meggy leves*—a chilled blend of morello cherries and sour cream. Roast goose and duck were included as well and *fogas*, a succulent freshwater fish from Lake Balaton, Europe's largest lake. My knowledge of all of this came from the running patter of Count Erich, who ate, drank, and talked with equal gusto throughout the mammoth meal.

We finally concluded our gluttony with several rounds of Tokaji Aszu, the syrupy wine with a taste reminiscent of bitter chocolate.

"That's it!" I declared as I pushed myself away from the tabletop carnage. "I'm not going to eat again ever!"

Gilda gave me a tantalizing look. "Not even if I put paprika on it?" she asked sultrily.

We were a considerably subdued band returning to the ship. Despite all the imbibing, no one was really intoxicated. The avalanche of food had turned a sea of alcohol into a sobering goulash. If anything, we were wearied by our overindulgence in the appetizing Hungarian cuisine. Slumber seemed temporarily more appealing than sex, a truly terrible state to be in.

The decks of the S.S. *Johann Sebastian* were awash with naked young women when we arrived, a testimonial to the success of Riddle's snatch safari. He was in the midst of it all, his formidable phallus sunk deeply into a diminutive black-tressed beauty who leaned over a lifeboat to accommodate him from the rear.

"How did it go?" I called out, a ridiculous question in view of the action abounding on all sides.

He grinned and made a victory "O" with his thumb and index finger. "The new theme of the cruise is 'Hump Hungarian!' " he proclaimed.

"Look at all the ass around here," Gilda observed with a measure of awe. "Are these hookers, or just sweet little neighborhood girls?"

"I don't know, but get the paprika and let's have a little dessert," I told her.

"I thought you were never going to eat again," she reminded me.

"This is not food, it's medication."

"Yes, doctor," she reacted with mock sarcasm. "Your degree in divine dimensions is finally coming in handy."

"I like coming in pussy better."

"Let's share a little hunk of Hungarian," Gilda suggested.

"There's enough here to have separate portions," I said, tugging at my clothes.

"Not when Erich, Ulrica and the others start digging in," she noted. "They just went to their cabins to strip."

We collaborated in ambushing a cute blonde

named Magda, who willingly submitted to an interior as well as exterior tongue bath from the two of us.

"Why do you choose me?" she questioned, fingering a cunt as multi-lipped as a fully petaled tulip.

"You just put your finger on the answer," I replied.

"My cuntie, cuntie?" she questioned teasingly.

"And your assie-assie and titty-titties," I elaborated.

"You like them?" she inquired, her fawnlike eyes opened wide.

"Like paprika," I responded.

Magda giggled so at my retort her entire curvy body jiggled.

"My nipples and my cunt, they are colored like paprika."

"That means they were meant to be eaten," Gilda joined in.

"Breakfast, lunch or dinner?" she asked coyly.

"All three meals," I replied, "seven days a week."

With that we both returned to lapping her luscious labia, the crevice of her derrière, her navel, her nipples, her mouth and her ears, sending her squirming in supreme sensuality. All about us everyone else was engaged in all manner of fellatio, fucking and cunnilingus, adding enormously to the ardor.

It might have gone on indefinitely had not Count Erich decided that enough was enough. The gluttony at dinner, followed by the gluttony on deck had left almost everyone physically stuffed and sexually sated.

"We have to take a vote," he reminded us as we bid adieus to the covey of curvaceous girls that Tommy and his cohorts had recruited from the streets of Budapest. "The time of decision is at hand."

Frankly, it no longer mattered to me what the outcome of the voting would be. I already knew the verdict regarding myself. This was, come hell or the Himalayas, my last night aboard the S.S. *Johann Sebastian.*

chapter twenty-six

Count Erich never got angry at me, but at first he was deeply disappointed that I intended to make Budapest my final stop on our reunion voyage.

"The vote was to continue," he said sadly the following morning.

"I abstained, in case you didn't notice."

"Of course I noticed, darling. I take note of everything you do, my little Nicole. But I assumed that was because you didn't want to be guilty of influencing the others."

"How could I do that? The graduates of the Académie Dumont are all of independent minds."

"They know this is really your voyage, your trip, as a special reunion gift from the countess and myself," he said softly.

"I suspected that," I replied with a twinge of remorse, "and I'm so grateful to you both for still another marvelous contribution to my life. But I'm exhausted now, dear count, and I really must go away to rest and recuperate. I'm amazed that you don't feel that same need yourself."

He smiled wanly.

"I'm probably twice as tired as you, sweet child," he admitted, "but I never want to let go of happiness. It's been such a heartwarming experience, taking part in the celebration of you and your former classmates."

"I realize that, and I'm touched by the joy you and Ulrica shared with us, but everything has to end sometime, and for me the time is now."

Gilda, who had been standing silently next to me, spoke up.

"I'm pulling out, too, Erich. It's been super-wonderful, but I'm strung out, just like Nicole. Maybe we're starting to get old."

The count laughed genuinely at her blithe observation.

"You are both still infants. It is I who am getting old." ·

It was our turn now to laugh.

"Not the way you were ringing those Budapest belles last night," I told him.

"Weren't they something?" he winked.

"There was just too much of everything to eat last night," Gilda noted.

Count Erich stood looking at the horizon now, his gentle face burnished by the morning sun. The Danube was mirror smooth, converting the sun's rays into a wide ribbon of diamonds. It was a beautiful morning and the river air cool and astringent. I should have been more tired considering the previous night's excesses, but instead I felt sparkingly alive and eager to get on with my future—whatever it held in store.

"So it is to be good-bye again, my darlings?" the count asked almost rhetorically.

"I'm afraid so, Erich," I replied for both of us.

There were tears in his soft brown eyes but his voice was calm and even.

"Go, then, with everlasting love and the prayer that *auf Wiedersehen* will be soon."

I embraced him tenderly, my own eyes misting.

"*Auf Wiedersehen*, dear count," I whispered in his ear.

Gilda was no less moved by the parting.

"Thank you again and again, Erich, for everything warm and wonderful you've done for me," she said in a choked voice as she hugged him.

We paid our respects to Ulrica in the same affectionate and affecting manner, this time allowing a few tears to fall.

"I feel like such a damned traitor," I confessed. "It seems so selfish of me to leave before it's all over."

"It is all over, dearest," Countess Ulrica said. "With you leaving, Erich has decided to cancel any further cruising."

"Now I feel even worse," I sobbed.

"Don't," she urged me. "It's really the best thing for every one. We needed someone with the courage to say 'Stop! We've had enough!' and you've done that for us, Nicole."

"Do you really mean that?" I asked hopefully.

"Absolutely. You should know that Erich never knows when to quit. We could be sailing all the rivers and seas of the world for years to come if we waited for him to make the decision to end the voyage."

"God bless you, Ulrica," I said. "You've made me feel so much better about it all."

"Go in love and good health—both of you. We'll be together again very soon."

Packing was so much more pleasant after the reassuring audience with the countess. She was such a kind and warm soul, so generous with herself in both body and spirit.

"What are your plans?" Gilda inquired as we stuffed our suitcases quickly.

"I'm calling Peter. A week or two on the Isle of Sappho is just what I needed to get my body and my mind back in synchronization."

"Good idea.

"What about you? Want to come with me?"

Gilda stopped packing for a moment and looked directly at me.

"That's sweet of you, Nicki, but I think we both need to be away from everything reminiscent of Académie Dumont for a while, including each other."

I smiled warmly at her.

"That's very honest of you," I said softly. "And it's also very right, too."

"I'll skip off to Rio again," she decided cheerily. "I always have a haven there."

"A heavenly haven," I laughed, immeasurably relieved by developments in the past hour, "just as I have with Peter."

"It's nice to know there's someone who's always there, isn't it?" she remarked.

"Peter Theophilus—dear to the gods and dearer still to me," I proclaimed.

I called Peter from the airport. As always, he was elated to hear from me and delighted at the prospect of my visiting him.

"I'd send my jet for you," he said excitedly, "but with the Communists, there's just too much hassle over landing permits. It would take weeks to get the necessary clearances."

"Don't worry about it. I'm happy hopping a

commercial flight to Athens. Maybe then I could use a lift to Sappho.''

''Your word is my command. Give me the landing details, and my man will be waiting for you.''

I spelled out the flight number, landing time, and airline for him.

''You've made not just my day, but my week, my month, my year!'' he rejoiced. ''And guess what?''

''What?''

''You've also given me a splendid erection,'' he laughed.

''Hold it until I get there,'' I urged him gaily.

''No, I'll build a fresh one for you—one that's even more spectacular.''

''I'll hold you to that promise,'' I declared.

''I'd rather you held *it.* ''

''Peter?''

''Yes, love?''

''I don't even want to see the yacht—much less go aboard it,'' I emphasized. ''I've had it with all ships for a while.''

''The *Nicole* looks beautiful, but I'll hide her in some harbor if you prefer.''

''Do,'' I urged him.

After I'd hung up, I experienced the most delicious sense of freedom and abandon I'd felt in weeks. It must have been visible because everyone in the terminal seemed to be staring at me as I skipped about, whistling and laughing, perceived no doubt as a capitalistic cuckoo escaped from a cage somewhere west of the Hungarian border.

Peter's efficiency was legendary, and nothing had changed since my last visit. Not only were plane and pilot exactly where they were supposed to be—and when they were supposed to be—but a couturier and a coiffeur were sent along to attend to my styling whims en route back to the island. A cassette recording, made by Peter himself, brought me up to date on all his business and recent personal activities. The signoff was indicative of his attention to detail.

"And so, Nicole, love of my life, I've brought you up to date on my life to this moment in order that we spend all of our time together dealing only with our present and our future. I wait with open arms to welcome you to me once more, to savor the succulence of your lips, the warm passion of your body, the beauty of you in every aspect. I await you on the veranda of the villa overlooking the sea. Come swiftly, my love . . . "

It was not simply another technological innovation on his part. Peter was essentially a romantic, despite his professional pragmatism. He loved his work as he loved me, the difference being that he could control the former but not the latter. How many times had I spurned his pleas to marry him—only to make his pursuit of me all the more ardently passionate?

It was too bad—for us both in different respects —that I could not accept the strictures of marriage. Peter would most likely be my choice if I were so inclined. But it was my devout intention never to be the bride of any man—or woman. I preferred to be just Nicole, a lone shooting star in the galaxy, leaving a luminous trail over the earth, shining brightly all the way to oblivion.

At any rate, I was genuinely happy to see him. He stood like a Greek god in a white linen suit and soft silk shirt, bronzed to perfection, his smile dazzling against the strong lines of his handsome face. The marble flooring of the patio was palatial and imparted a regal air to his bearing. I felt mo-

mentarily like a princess returning to her Prince
Charming.

"Pe-tah," I uttered in my best Bette Davis
fashion as I rushed to him.

"My love," he whispered as he swept me into
his strong arms.

We stood with lips merged for long moments
before speaking again. He held me at arm's length
several times, his eyes swimming over my body,
and then drew me to his mouth again. It was a
ritual of which we never tired, re-enacted at each
reunion.

"The only way I can bear being parted from
you," he confessed, "is knowing how sweet it will
be when you return."

"I've missed you," I told him sincerely.

"You've been too busy," he demurred.

"Never for thoughts of you."

"Those are very provocative words."

"I get that strong impression," I teased, drawing my crotch away momentarily from the press of
his prick.

"You're terribly tantalizing, Nicole."

"Is that a complaint?"

"It's a plaintive desire to come," he punned.

"Far be it from me to deny a friend salvation,"
I replied, unhooking my dress so that it slid down
my body and onto the marble deck. In that instant
I rendered myself totally naked except for my
shoes and bracelet.

"How angelic!" he gasped. "You're a vision—
an absolute vision!"

"I'm a devil with an incision," I countered.
"Fill me with yourself, Peter, and let's be truly,
totally together."

He needed no further encouragement. His
aesthetic appraisal of me soon turned to savage

fucking, with cannibalistic overtones. Primitive grunts and hungry nibbling accompanied his burrowing into the bung of my box.

"Nobody fucks like you," he told me, his breath hot against my neck. "Nobody anywhere."

"You cocksucker!" I said searingly, "you lying sonofabitch!"

Peter hardened perceptibly as a result of my profane patter.

"I'd like to fuck your ass till you bleed, you cunt-loving bitch!" he retaliated.

Out on the terrace, under the afternoon sun, we were oblivious to everything and everyone as we strove together to attain the summit of orgasmic sexuality.

"Fuck me, you fucking fairy!" I shrieked.

The accusation really aroused him, knowing that I knew of his penchant for feminine lingerie.

"You asshole dike bitch!" he snarled in response, fucking me now like a berserk pile driver. "Call me a fucking fag—I'll drown your fucking whore's pussy with come!"

The lingo had us both stretched so taut it seemed that every fiber in our bodies was ready to snap. My nipples were hard as rubies and my cunt as tense as a drumhead. I could feel the veins of Peter's prick as it set fire to the tinder of my box.

"Come with me!" I pleaded, seconds before succumbing to a mammoth deluge from within and without.

He had not needed my encouragement to produce such a glut of oysterish semen it overflowed the well of my womb and left small, luminous pearls decorating the cornsilk of my cunt.

I licked him clean and in the process drew out his reserves of come in another spectacular climax. He then did the same for me, tasting himself in the hollow of my haunches before sending me off on another flight of ecstasy.

"How was it," he questioned slyly as we rested on a chaise, "considering I'm a faggot?"

I reached over and petted his briefly flaccid cock.

"You're the best fucking fag a woman could want," I answered impishly, my *cunt*entment quite complete—and quite obvious as well.

chapter twenty-seven

In the cocoon of Lesbos, which I always preferred
to call the Isle of Sappho, I found the peace I was
seeking. Peter's place was just above Polyknitos,
overlooking the majestic bay and the Aegean Sea.
I could spread myself there like some great bird
sunning its wings. My own gamebird soaked up
the sun with the same spread-eagled spirit of *sans
souci* as the real feathered flock that called the
island home.

"A beautiful piece at peace," Peter observed
with obvious satisfaction.

"I love it here. If I ever decide to nest, it'll be
right here."

"I'd love to lay my eggs in your nest."

I lay back and thought about the reunion, about
the cruise, and about everyone I loved. It was
wonderful to be so accepted, so adored, so pur-
sued. But it was also marvelous to be in the company of only one individual at a time—one man in
this case who worshiped the ground I fucked on.

"Peter," I said softly, "you are so special to me that it's almost frightening."

"Let me scare you even more," he said with a certain air of sangfroid, "I have a new secretary who's very special to me."

"That's frightening?" I reacted.

"Not on the surface. Below the surface."

"Below the navel, in other words?"

"Make your own decision after the introduction," he replied, an unusually enigmatic response from him.

With a flair for the dramatic, he slid open the floor-to-ceiling glass panels of his solarium, touched a button to send the ivory draperies dancing aside in a majestic swirl, and then announced her name as though introducing a star.

"Peter Theophilus, Ltd., takes pride and pleasure in introducing the new private secretary to the chairman of the board and chief executive officer, the irrepressible and irresistible Robin Manor . . ."

What a come-on, I thought to myself. Had Peter overdosed on executive sweets, was he spaced out on Dow Jones averages or was he just having a bit of uncommon flaky fun at my expense? But one look at the young lady in question made it appear unlikely that it was all a joke. She was nothing short of scrumptious.

"Robin," Peter said as she eased erotically onto the patio, "this is my darling Nicole."

The raven-tressed beauty, with hair spilling all the way down to her impressive tits, spread her lips open slowly in vulval fashion, licking them sensually before deigning to speak.

"Hello, darling Nicole," she responded, slowly and sultrily.

"Robin, how are you? I'm certainly impressed by Peter's talent in personnel selection."

"He's a simply mahvelous employer," she declared, her obviously British accent becoming more pronounced with each utterance.

"I found her in London, working in a club in Soho," Peter volunteered.

"That is a first-rate secretarial pool," I observed with good-natured sarcasm.

Robin ignored the jape. "Peter tells me you're a graduate of the Académie Dumont," she said, her eyes disrobing me with their carnal intensity.

"Yes, I just came from a reunion to end all reunions."

"Is it still such a staid school?"

I couldn't resist smiling at that. "Only on the surface. The reunion made it seem more like a college for concubines."

"Really? That surprises me. I was expelled from there for doing nothing more than baring my soul."

"Robin is *all* soul," Peter inserted playfully.

He was much more relaxed around her than I'd ever seen him be with any of his other female employees.

"I can't imagine Dr. Beauregard allowing a woman of your looks to be thrown out of his school," I commented.

"Maybe I can illustrate the main reason," Robin said with an air of mystery. "Would you suggest that, Peter?"

"I think that would be an excellent idea."

"Here?" she asked.

Peter glanced about the wide open terrace, populated only with large plants and plumply cushioned patio furniture.

"Why not? We have only the sun of God looking on."

I watched entranced as Robin moved gracefully and provocatively to center stage—the open middle of the terrace where a small fountain flowed, spewing frothy white water from the penis and vagina of twin marble statues. She chose to do her thing directly in front of the figures, a most appropriate spot as it turned out.

"Nicole," Peter said standing next to me, "keep in mind Robin's surname as you watch her."

I eyed him quizzically. "Manor?" I questioned.

Peter nodded as his secretary began displaying her assets if not her skills as yet. And what an asset she had—a prominent but perfectly proportioned posterior with a devastating divide down the middle that showed through the clinging translucence of her dress. In true Greek tradition, Peter was an ardent admirer of amorous asses. If the truth were told, I probably had a strain of Greek running in my ancestry since I was also captivated by a well-lathed rump.

"I can see the kind of dictation she takes," I told Peter. "Just look at the early effect on your dick."

Peter did not take his smoky gray eyes off her to acknowledge my observation. Instead he merely confirmed the condition of his cock by placing his hand upon it in a form of blessing.

"You're going to like her," he predicted. "She grows on you."

"She doesn't have to grow on me," I replied, warming up to the occasion. "She just has to get on me and get me off."

A smile flickered on his face.

"Cool it awhile," he advised, obviously pleased at my reaction.

"I thought I needed reunion recuperation, and here I am looking for copulation again instead."

Robin shook her head like a wild colt, sending her lustrous mane of anthracite hair flying like a cloud of midnight. Her nostrils flared and her body gleamed as she sprung her huge tits loose, their nipples like ripe plums on mounds of cream pudding.

"Damn!" she yelped gleefully, a joyous celebration of her marvelous mammaries.

"You must get a lot of work done with those tits in your face all the time," I kidded Peter.

"Everything gets accomplished via the milky way," he joked in response.

Robin leaned over, her ass in our direction, letting the spray from the fountain sprinkle her imposing chest. She wiggled and writhed as the misty water turned her wet-nursing potential even wetter.

"This is like a show-business performance," I noted.

"It's what she was doing when I found her," Peter explained. "I encourage her to keep up with her acting and dancing along with the business end of things."

"Her business end is right there at the end of her spine," I observed with a trace of sardonic sophism.

Peter did not disagree. He was caught up in the tease of her slow, sensual strip, his prick standing out in bas relief against the front of his slacks.

"Watch this," he urged me as though I could possibly be distracted by something else.

"If my eyes pop out any farther, you can play marbles with them."

"Now," he said as she wheeled around after discarding all but the lacy black panties guarding her groin.

"What a meaty cunt she must have," I uttered almost involuntarily.

Both of her hands formed a "V" over the triangle of her crotch as she hooked her thumbs into the elastic of the briefs, ready to pull them down. It was as though she had a wild animal trapped there, ready to spring to freedom the moment she removed her hands.

"Are you ready, willing and able, Nicole?" Robin inquired throatily.

"To suck and to fuck!" I declared with passion.

"Fuck you, then!" Robin cried, throwing her hands over her head after yanking down the panties.

I gasped at what I saw before me—a full, fat, bone-hard prick that stood like an arrow pointing upward at her proud and provocative tits.

"Robin Manor!" I shrieked.

"Man or woman," Peter clarified his earlier remark. "Take your choice."

"Fuck me while I suck your sweet melons, my baby!" I cried out with abandon.

"Let me at that honey hole, darling," Robin retorted, waiting impatiently for me to tear off the last of my clothes.

"I've got some tasty, rare cock for you to eat while you're doing it," Peter told his secretary as he/she aimed the swollen arrow at the heart of my haunches.

As a new staff acquisition I found no way to fault Robin Manor. She could give and take dick —if not dictation—with the best of her breed, and in legendary Greek tradition, she gave it to her boss as well as to me.

What transpired transsexually that afternoon was the stuff that myths are made of—whether with a myth or mythter. We did everything but lisp as we licked and laid one another all over the terrace, even adding our own golden contributions to the pissing pair of statues in the bubbling fountain. Peter insisted on a fashion show before dinner, one in which he and Robin collaborated in modeling the latest and lewdest in lacy lingerie. There was even a delicate beribboned sack for tying up one's balls, should one be so endowed. Finally, thankfully, for the time being, we agreed to dine on something more substantial and nutritious than the savory but non-nourishing juices and syrups of crotch flesh.

Peter was in a relaxed and exuberant mood after dinner. With Robin returned to the *Nicole* to monitor the overseas stock reports in the chartroom there, we walked hand-in-hand by the side of the sea, talking of tomorrow, dreaming different dreams but sharing the sweet joy of being together again, fond friends forever.

Watch for

NICOLE FOLLOWS THE SUN

next in the NICOLE series
coming in November!

Nicole

Morgan St. Michel

She's a woman made for every conceivable act of love, schooled to sinful perfection in the erotic arts, a ravenous and infinitely giving mistress who lives to gratify her senses — and her readers!!

___ NICOLE	06345-2/$2.95
___ NICOLE IN FLIGHT	06346-0/$2.95
___ NICOLE IN CAPTIVITY	06347-9/$2.95
___ NICOLE'S SUMMER PLEASURES	06891-8/$2.95
___ NICOLE'S REUNION	07132-3/$2.95
___ A CARNIVAL FOR NICOLE	06647-8/$2.95
___ NICOLE'S PRIVATE DIARY	07113-7/$2.95
___ NICOLE TOUCHES THE STARS	07063-7/$2.95
___ NICOLE AT THE GRAND PRIX	07084-X/$2.95

CHRISTINA
AN EXCITING SERIES OF ELEGANT EROTICA